Walker moved behind her and slid his arms around her waist.

Everything inside her went still.

"What are you doing?"

"Helping with the dishes."

More like helping mow down her last remaining defenses.

Jen knew she should tell him to move or step away herself, but she couldn't. He felt too good. The warm spice of his dark masculine scent had her wanting to turn and bury her face in his neck.

As they rinsed off the suds, he nuzzled his stubbled jaw against her cheek. Every nerve ending popped and the heat she'd felt all night edged into need.

"Man, you smell good," he breathed. "I just want to eat you up."

"Okay," she said dazedly. A faint voice warned she wasn't supposed to agree like that.

Dear Reader,

Some heroes just get you *right there*. For me,
Walker McClain is one of those guys. Tall. Gorgeous.
Broodingly sexy.

Walker last appeared on the page at his brother's wedding,
and that night he fell in love. In short order, he got
everything he ever wanted—a beautiful wife, a baby on the
way and a job as a firefighter and SWAT medic. He still has
the job, but two and a half years ago his wife and unborn
child were murdered during a brutal mugging by someone
witnesses described as a homeless man. Over the past six
months, several homeless men have been killed and set on
fire. The cops' prime suspect? Walker McClain.

Firefighter Jen Lawson snags the assignment to go
undercover and find out if the murder of Walker's wife
transformed him into a vigilante. She's touched by the
devotion Walker felt for his wife and knocked off balance
by an intense attraction to him. Still, Jen is determined to do
her job…without falling for the man who might be a killer.

Since Walker first appeared in *Melting Point,* I've gotten
a lot of mail from readers asking for his story. I hope you
enjoy it.

Warmly,

Debra Cowan

DEBRA COWAN

The Vigilante Lover

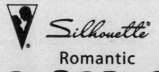

Silhouette®

Romantic

SUSPENSE

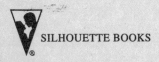

SILHOUETTE BOOKS

ISBN-13: 978-0-373-27668-4

THE VIGILANTE LOVER

Copyright © 2010 by Debra S. Cowan

Visit Silhouette Books at www.eHarlequin.com

Printed in U.S.A.

Books by Debra Cowan

Silhouette Romantic Suspense
Dare to Remember #774
The Rescue of Jenna West #858
One Silent Night #899
Special Report #1045
 "Cover Me!"
Still the One #1127
*Burning Love #1236
*Melting Point #1370
*Wild Fire #1404
*The Private Bodyguard #1593
*The Vigilante Lover #1598

*The Hot Zone

DEBRA COWAN

Like many writers, Debra made up stories in her head
as a child. Her B.A. in English was obtained with the
intention of following family tradition and becoming a
schoolteacher, but after she wrote her first novel, there
was no looking back. After years of working another job
in addition to writing, she now devotes herself full-time
to penning both historical and contemporary romances.
An avid history buff, Debra enjoys traveling. She has
visited places as diverse as Europe and Honduras, where
she and her husband served as part of a medical mission
team. Born in the foothills of the Kiamichi Mountains,
Debra still lives in her native Oklahoma with her
husband and their two beagles, Maggie and Domino.

Debra invites her readers to contact her at P.O. Box
30123, Coffee Creek Station, Edmond, OK 73003-0003
or via e-mail at her Web site, www.debracowan.net.

ACKNOWLEDGMENTS

Many thanks to Cody Goodnight for answering my questions about firefighter and paramedic procedures. You were a tremendous help!

Chapter 1

Presley firefighter Walker McClain did his best to slip back unnoticed into his firehouse, which was tricky considering the entire crew was gathered in an empty engine bay. It helped that everyone in the loose circle had their backs to him and that all three bay doors were open.

It was straight-up 7:00 a.m. on the first twenty-four hours of his new shift. He wasn't late, but like the other firefighters he typically reported for work ten or fifteen minutes early, and people would notice that today he hadn't. He'd spent two of his four days off working on his "obsession," as his brother called it.

Even this early in the morning, September in Oklahoma had plenty of heat and humidity. Walker moved all the way inside Station House Three. Thumbing a bead of sweat from his temple, he eased up next to his buddy, Dylan Shepherd.

He could feel Shep's steely gaze on him and kept his own

attention fixed straight ahead on Captain Yearwood and the dark-haired woman beside him. He wasn't telling Shep where he'd been. He didn't want to see the looks or hear the questions.

"What's going on?" he asked quietly.

Shep inclined his head toward the woman. "Her. That's what."

And she did have it going on, Walker admitted reluctantly. Even the PFD's standard uniform of navy blue pants and a crisp, light blue shirt couldn't conceal her sleek, tight curves. His gaze skimmed down her body, then took a much slower trip on the way back up. Long legs, slender hips, breasts that would just fit his—

"Everybody, meet Jen Lawson," Captain Yearwood boomed, to be heard over the occasional street noise coming in through the open bay doors. He gestured to the group of seven firefighters, indicating the only other female on their shift, Shelby Fox Jessup. "You've met Jessup."

The women exchanged smiles.

"Next to her is Farris, then Shepherd and McClain." The captain, a lean man with gray hair and sharp, dark eyes, glanced at Walker. "McClain, you'll want to get with Lawson."

What the hell for?

"She's transferring over from Tulsa," the man was saying. "Filling the spot Pickett left when he retired."

His muscles went tight. "So, you're a SWAT medic, too?"

"Yes. Nice to meet you." Her gaze fully lined up with his for the first time and Walker went stupid for about half a second.

Wow. Her eyes were stunning, a pure, hot blue. He had never seen such an intense shade.

Captain Yearwood, who'd transferred to Station House

Three a little more than three years ago, continued introductions around the loose circle of firefighters who made up the blue shift.

Walker didn't have to wait more than two seconds for Farris, the company Casanova, to chime in. Tall and built like a brick wall, the burly man kept his voice low, for Walker's and Shep's ears only. "I gotta have her."

Ass. "You might want to wait until you see if she can cover your back at a fire."

"If she can't, I bet she can cover my front just fine."

Walker didn't waste his breath pointing out that if overheard, Farris could be reported for sexual harassment. The muscled-up blond man moved around the circle to get closer to the brunette.

Shep groaned under his breath. "I think I'm in love. Did you see those eyes?"

He had.

"That face?"

Yes.

"And did you see her body?"

"No, I've gone blind in the last five seconds," Walker drawled. Hell, yes, he'd seen it. And noticing so much about her irritated him.

"Aren't you interested at all? It's been over two years, man. You didn't die that night."

No, but Walker wished he had. Ever since Holly had expired in his arms, he had felt like an empty black pit inside. He hadn't lost only his wife to that brutal mugging; he'd lost their unborn daughter, too. Sometimes he felt every one of those days all over again.

As the captain dismissed them, Walker started past the other firefighters, heading for the kitchen as he said to Shep, "It's my turn to cook. I gotta check the groceries."

Since Holly's murder, he had been trying to find the SOB who'd done it. Even after two and a half years, all he had to go on was a vague physical description of a homeless man with a knife scar across the knuckles of his right hand.

For a while, he'd given up hope of ever getting any further, but six months ago someone had started killing homeless men. Burning them. So far, there were three victims, and they were all repeat offenders of violent crimes. Scumbags who had been released after serving their time and had shown no signs of stopping their behavior, who were past the point of rehabilitation.

On the chance one of the dead men was the man Walker was searching for, he had been paying close attention to the recent victims. His brother, Collier, might consider Walker's investigation an obsession, but Walker didn't care.

"McClain?"

The slightly husky feminine voice at his back had him turning to the newest member of their shift.

Jen Lawson's skin was a creamy pink and white. The black hair she'd pulled back into a braid looked thick, wavy. Her perfect lips curved. "Where should I leave my blow-out pack?"

"On your tactical vest. And leave that with your other gear." The SWAT medics carried their pouch of medical supplies on every call. They were firefighters first and SWAT medics when needed. "We may not need our turnout gear on a SWAT call, but having everything in one place makes it easier to grab and go, in case we do."

"Thanks."

She stood close enough that he could smell her now—a musky, floral fragrance that made his body tighten. And his voice. "Have you checked in with the SWAT team?"

"Earlier this morning, before I reported here."

Her eyes were incredible, emphasized even more by a slight widow's peak and the delicate arch of dark eyebrows. Her oval face and defined cheekbones made her appear dainty. She looked almost too slight to make a difference on the fire line.

It took a second for Walker to realize she'd walked away and he was standing there staring stupidly after her, as if he'd run into a wall. Cursing under his breath, he stepped into the kitchen and around the long, scratched dining table. Lawson hadn't done anything except ask him a question, and his blood was humming. What was that about?

Just as he reached the refrigerator, the alarm sounded. He bolted to the bay along with everyone else, suited up and jumped on the engine.

With Captain Yearwood driving, they reached the scene less than ten minutes later. It was an abandoned house north of Benson Street, an industrial area of town with several warehouses. A quick glance around showed there were no bystanders yet. Orange flames shot into the sky over a dilapidated white frame house, already partially engulfed.

As a fire engine and a ladder truck from Station Two, Walker's old firehouse, parked behind them, he and his crew were off their engine and pulling hose. House fires typically had two stations responding, along with the station that housed the rescue truck.

Luckily, the wind wasn't hampering their efforts so far. He tuned in to the crackling hiss of the fire, the thunk of the hydrant valve as the main line was attached, the initial roar of water as it gushed through the hose.

Upon entry, they found no one inside. The crews poured water on the burning structure. Dark gray smoke turned to white when the water hit it, all of it mixing into a billowing gunmetal cloud against the blue sky.

It didn't take long to extinguish the flames, and Walker had a good guess as to why. The house hadn't been where the fire started. He would bet his OU season football tickets the blaze had been caused by the burning of a body, and the flames had moved from the victim to the wooden building.

The scenes of the other Payback Killer victims had also been quickly put out, and a body burned by flashbangs had turned up at each one.

Once the blaze was doused, they checked for hot spots and found none. Satisfied the fire was truly out, Walker took off his helmet and Nomex hood. Around him, the other firefighters did the same.

Beneath his turnout coat, his navy T-shirt was soaked with sweat, and the acrid stench of burned wood and chemicals settled around him. The torched dwelling was the only remaining house on a street that had been bought by a commercial developer. With the sun shining down on the charred and smoldering structure, the place looked desolate.

Gray smoke plumed into the air. Water from the hoses flowed down the streets and saturated the unkempt brown grass.

Walker trudged to the back of the house through the scraggly yard now turned to mud. He expected to see a burned body, and he did. "Body back here, Captain!"

He crouched, his gaze taking in the bubbled flesh on the side of the victim's face, the heat-bloated skin on his hands and arms. The bodies were never burned beyond recognition, just used as a human fuse to send the flames to the house and trigger a call to 911. Walker had time before the others joined him to check the dead man's right hand. No knife scar across his knuckles. This man wasn't Holly's killer.

Shep and Lawson appeared. Yearwood trotted toward them from the engine.

Remaining several feet away from the body, Shep glanced at Walker. "The Payback Killer?"

His gaze landed on the flashbang close to the victim. Jaw tight, Walker nodded. Only the back half of the house was burned away, which was in keeping with his theory that the blaze had spread from the incinerated body. If the house had been the target, the fire would've been set to do much more damage.

The remaining frame looked as if it might crumble any second. The familiar odor of scorched wood and engine fumes hung heavy in the air. As Walker brushed away the ash that grazed his cheek, he noticed Lawson staring quietly at their John Doe. Her gaze shifted to the flashbang and she frowned.

Farris joined them, tossing bottles of cold water to her, Walker and Shep. "Wanna bet that crispy corpse has a record?"

"Yeah, just like the other ones." Shep, sans helmet and hood, dumped his bottle of water over his head to cool off, then dragged a hand down his face.

Lawson glanced at Walker. "The Payback Killer? What are y'all talking about? What other ones? How many other ones?"

In response, he took a long drink of cold water.

But Shep didn't hesitate. "If this body checks out to be like the others, this will be the fourth murder victim who's a repeat offender, a *violent* offender who served his time or was recently released from prison for good behavior or some other reason."

"So, the Payback Killer is a vigilante," she said.

"Yeah." Shep pointed toward the street, where Station Two's engine and the rescue truck were parked. "There's Marshal Burke."

Walker tracked Tom Burke's progress as the big black man

made his way toward the battalion chief in charge of the scene.

Lawson's eyebrows rose. "The state fire marshal is handling this?"

Walker knew she was wondering what the rest of them had wondered when they'd learned the case had been turned over from the Presley fire investigators to the state. Was someone in the fire department a suspect?

The firefighters knew the cops were looking for one suspect who was believed to be preying on the homeless, but there was nothing to indicate they or Fire Chief Wheat believed that suspect was someone in the fire department.

After the second murder, everyone at Walker's station house had been questioned. Had they noticed anyone hanging around the neighborhood who looked out of place? Had they seen anyone harassing the homeless men or paying them an undue amount of attention? But those were routine questions that would be asked of anyone located close to the shelter where all the homeless victims had stayed at least once.

Most likely, the case had been transferred to avoid claims of prejudice in the investigation. Understandable, considering Presley's fire investigators had once been its firefighters—not to mention one of the current FIs was Walker's brother.

"And there's Jack Spencer." Shep glanced at Lawson, indicating the tall detective who'd just gotten out of his car, parked at the curb in front of the rescue truck. "Procedure between Presley's fire and police departments dictates the cops have to be called if a body is found in a fire. We put out the blaze, then call Homicide. Spencer and one other detective are the ones assigned to the Payback Killer case. If Jack's here, they must think this death is related to the others."

Lawson turned to Walker. "Do you think the victim burned up? Or was he dead before the fire started?"

"That's for the M.E. to figure out." He didn't know why she was asking him when Shep was spilling info left and right. Walker poured some water into his hand and rubbed it across his heat-scalded nape.

Shep continued, "It was determined the other victims died before the fires. And all of them had traces of magnesium and ammonium perchlorate on their bodies."

Lawson frowned. "Those chemicals are metal powders found in flashbangs."

Walker wasn't surprised she knew that. She would've learned it in her SWAT training.

"So flashbangs are being used as an accelerant?"

"Yeah." Shep went on to explain that six months ago, a case of the stun grenades had been stolen out of the SWAT van. A key was required to get into the van, and it had been kept locked unless a member of the team was inside. Only certain people had access to the key. All of the SWAT team. And the SWAT medics.

"Why are you using the word *victims* for this scum?" Farris snapped. "These SOBs aren't victims. Those other three had it coming and this one probably did, too."

Lawson's eyes widened.

Walker knew how vengeful Farris sounded, but he felt the same way. As he and the other firefighters returned to the front of the property, he realized he was staring at Lawson. Beneath the grime, he could see her skin was as fine-grained as silk. He dragged his gaze from the streak of soot on her cheek, the sheen of perspiration on her neck.

He and the others joined Farris and they began to refold the main hose.

"It's hard to care much about these bastards getting back some of what they've dished out," Farris bit out.

"Even though the M.O. is the same as that of the Payback Killer, we aren't certain yet that this victim is a violent offender. I guess there's a chance this could've been done by a copycat. Regardless, we should stop talking and get this cleaned up," Walker said. "Monroe's setting up the portable floodlights inside the house for the fire marshal, and St. George from Station Two is videotaping the scene."

He could feel Lawson's gaze on him and figured she had more questions. She could ask Shep since he seemed to be bleeding answers this afternoon.

"Do you videotape all your scenes?" she asked. "In Tulsa, we did about ninety percent of the time, especially if we thought the blaze was suspicious."

Farris muttered something Walker didn't catch. Shep walked to the back of the engine with Lawson, answering her question and further explaining Presley Fire Department policy.

Walker could hear the low huskiness of her voice and did his best to keep his attention from her. She'd done good work this afternoon. He liked the way she handled herself, he admitted grudgingly. Regardless of her appearance—or maybe in spite of it—she'd held her own, put her head down along with the rest of them and killed the blaze.

She moved quickly though not sloppily, was friendly to the guys but didn't flirt. She obviously took her job seriously.

Her looks were deceiving. There was a tenacity underneath all that gorgeousness.

He wondered why she'd moved to Presley. If she was married or involved with anyone. He caught himself before he thought further. Why did he even care? He worked with her and that was it.

* * *

Walker McClain was her man, and he was more than Jen had expected. He was more compelling, more attractive, just…more.

She had his file, but the general details there did little to describe the flesh-and-blood man. Tall and lean, he was rangy, with solid wiry muscles. What no personnel photo could show was the intensity of his dusky green eyes. Or the deep dimples that had flashed once. His seal-dark hair was thick and slightly shaggy, his jaw stubbled with whiskers. Walker McClain was a great-looking guy, and Jen had felt a tug of flat-out lust low in her belly when their eyes met. It startled her.

A searing awareness had settled under her skin. She didn't like it, but she could deal with it. Part of every assignment was figuring out how the suspect operated and knowing this early that McClain affected her would help her keep up her guard.

She didn't need any help keeping up her guard around her other suspect. Brett Farris rubbed her the wrong way. Still, she had to confirm or eliminate him as a possible culprit.

It was almost nine o'clock the next evening when she parked at the far corner of a crowded Oklahoma City amusement park off I-35. Making her way two rows over, she slipped into the backseat of a dark blue SUV, greeting the people inside. Beside her sat Jack Spencer, the lean, handsome detective whom she'd seen at the fire scene yesterday. In the driver's seat was Fire Marshal Tom Burke, whom Jen had pretended not to know when Shep had pointed him out at the fire scene yesterday. Also up front was Robin Daly, a petite brunette who was the other Presley detective assigned to this case.

Aside from her and Fire Chief Wheat, these people were the only ones who knew about the covert investigation. All the chief knew was that someone was working undercover, but not who.

Jen's first twenty-four-hour shift was over, and she was free until the following morning at seven. Despite the vehicle's air-conditioning, her hands were sweating. She wasn't sure if it was due to the risk of the job or the man she was supposed to primarily investigate.

She'd been thinking a lot about that man. The fine lines around McClain's eyes indicated he laughed a lot. Or used to. She'd caught a glimpse of something hard behind his easy smile. Understandable, considering he'd lost his wife of less than one year and their unborn daughter.

Jen's heart twisted and she gave herself a mental shake.

Emotion had no place in this type of work and she was extremely conscious of that, had been since her rookie undercover assignment in Tulsa, when she'd gotten too close to someone who had been implicated in her investigation. But it wasn't only her job that had taught her how to turn off her feelings. She'd also learned with Mark.

Toward the end of their engagement, when her fiancé hadn't recognized her for long stretches at a time, Jen had felt as though her heart was being ripped out every time she saw him. Distancing herself had been difficult, almost devastating, but it had ultimately saved her sanity. That swell of emotion, the connection she'd felt with McClain yesterday, was a warning and she intended to listen.

Realizing the fire marshal had asked her a question, she shifted her focus to him. "I don't have much yet," she said. "I'm settling in."

"But you've met him?" Burke asked in his deep resonant voice.

"Yes. The captain introduced me around to everyone at the same time. McClain showed up at seven sharp, not several minutes early the way the rest of us did, including Farris."

Spencer's eyes narrowed. "McClain arrived just in time to respond to yesterday's fire murder?"

Jen nodded. The detective had obviously noted McClain's presence at the scene.

"About how long before the alarm did he get to the firehouse?" Daly asked.

"Maybe five or six minutes. I don't know yet where he was or how long he was gone."

"So there's an unspecified window of time that he could've used to kill the victim then torch him."

"Depending on what the medical examiner estimates as time of death, it's possible."

Spencer spoke up. "It'll be tricky to get as close to him as you may need to. If you were cops, you could partner up."

"It helps that you're both SWAT medics," Daly pointed out. "There will be calls the two of you will respond to without the others."

Jen had considered that, after she'd gotten a little distance from McClain.

Draping one big hand over the steering wheel, Burke angled his shoulder against the driver's-side window. "What's your impression so far?"

"He's dedicated to his job, respects others who are the same."

"Is our only evidence on him still circumstantial?"

"Yes," both detectives replied.

The fire marshal's sharp gaze panned over them. "McClain's wife being murdered by a homeless man gives him more motive than anyone to kill these people."

"More motive than anyone we know about," Jen emphasized.

Daly nodded. "Right. And with zero physical evidence that he killed anyone, we can't interview him."

"He's made no secret of the fact he's still searching for his wife's killer," Burke said. "Or that he intends to make them pay."

"I just don't know if he would take the law into his own hands," Robin said.

Spencer's quiet voice was grim. "If my wife and daughter had been murdered and the cops didn't have a lead after two and a half years, I can't say what I would do."

Burke glanced at Jen. "McClain has motive, and he regularly visits homeless shelters, supposedly looking for his wife's killer."

"And those visits could also be used to select the next Payback Killer victim," she speculated.

"Could be. We also know he has the means to commit these murders."

"Yes, but he isn't the only one with legitimate access to the flashbangs that have been used by the killer."

"Even so," Daly said, "we haven't been able to find anyone else with motive to kill these people. So far our digging hasn't turned up a connection between any SWAT team member and the Payback Killer."

"We're still looking at all the guys at Station House Three," Burke said.

Jen nodded. "The other person on our radar is Brett Farris. His volunteering every week with his church at the homeless shelter has put him in contact with all our victims and maybe given him inside knowledge of who these men really were."

"But that's all we have on him," the fire marshal observed.

Jen frowned. "Just because he doesn't have *authorized* access to the flashbangs used by SWAT doesn't mean he couldn't get to them if he wanted to badly enough. When that case of grenades was stolen, the van wasn't broken into; it was unlocked. Someone could've gotten their hands on a key to the SWAT van and made a copy."

Burke's dark eyes glittered in the wash of floodlight coming into the SUV. "You said you didn't see McClain at the firehouse until minutes before the alarm? Did anyone else?"

"I talked to the rest of the crew. No one recalls seeing him there before I did."

"How did he act at the scene?" Daly asked.

Jen wiped a clammy hand down her jeans-clad thigh. "I didn't see any truly suspicious behavior. Farris and another firefighter filled me in on the murders. They all share the opinion that the Payback Killer should be allowed to continue wiping scum from the face of the earth, but McClain didn't weigh in on any of it. He wouldn't talk about the murders, period. He barely talked to *me*. The only question of mine he responded to was about time of death and he said the M.E. would be the one with answers."

"He didn't express an opinion at all?" Burke asked.

"Not to me." She hesitated then said, "He did go straight to the body, as though he already knew where it was."

Spencer's gaze sliced to her. "Did he do anything to it?" She shook her head. "No, just looked."

"And now we know from the victim's fingerprints he was a repeat violent offender," Jack said. "So this murder is now officially a Payback Killer case."

Burke was quiet for a moment. "You're off to a good start, Lawson. We'll meet again after your next shift and see if you've learned anything."

Jen nodded and slid out of the SUV, her mind still on Walker as she made her way back to her car. He had definitely rattled her cage, sparked an immediate response inside her she had never felt on the job. Purely a woman-to-man response.

Enough of a response to have all Jen's feminine instincts blaring at her to stay away from the guy, but she didn't have that option. Her only option was to work the case.

She didn't have a problem with these repeat violent offenders getting punished, but she did have a problem with it being outside the law.

Had the death of McClain's wife and child turned him into a vigilante? Into the Payback Killer? She was here to find out.

Chapter 2

The next evening, Jen's instincts were still screaming at her, and she hadn't even gotten within ten feet of McClain. But she would. She had to.

She'd been watching him all day. During two firehouse tours with elementary-school kids and at the training center, as everyone practiced driving the new engine bought with federal grant money they'd been awarded a few months ago.

Now she paused in the doorway to the kitchen, a rectangular room dominated by a long table in the middle. The floor was cement, and light oak cabinets lined two walls in an L-shape. She took a moment to study McClain before he saw her.

He stood across the room near the sink, which was in the middle of the shorter length of counter. His red T-shirt, with Presley Fire Department stamped on the back in white letters, was untucked. An occasional tapping noise coming from his direction told her he was chopping something.

With each movement of his arm, muscle flexed beneath the cotton. The shirt stretched across strong broad shoulders, then fell from the trim line of his waist to a pair of faded jeans that fit so well Jen's gaze lingered on his backside longer than it should have.

He was double-dip delicious with his lean build and green eyes and a shadow of whiskers on a jaw that seemed to lock every time she looked at him. His dark, ragged hair brushed the collar of his T-shirt and she wanted to sink her hands into its thickness.

Good freakin' grief!

She wasn't here to get close to him that way. She was here to find out if he was a cold-blooded killer. Shaking off her ridiculous thoughts, she walked into the kitchen and skirted the dining table. Padded brown folding chairs were strung in a disorderly line down both sides.

She stopped at the refrigerator, which occupied the space at the end of the long counter broken up only by a large stove in the same stainless-steel finish. "Hey."

McClain's shoulders stiffened and he glanced over his shoulder, waving a wicked-looking knife in her direction. "You shouldn't sneak up on people."

"Sorry. I was going to make some tea. Should I come back?"

"No." He glanced at the clock on the far wall. "Supper's in about an hour. How about making enough for everybody?"

"Sure. I make sweet tea. Is that all right?"

"Do two dispensers of sweetened and two of unsweetened. The containers are in that cabinet by your knee."

"All right."

He turned back to a cutting board and Jen opened the door he'd indicated. Spying several large plastic beverage dispensers, she took four then began searching for tea bags.

"Tea's in the second cabinet on the top," McClain offered. "Pots and pans are on my side of the stove."

"Thanks." She moved over next to him and bent to look inside the cabinet. Taking two of the largest pots, she stepped around him to the sink and began filling the first one.

This close, she could smell man and soap and a faint dark spice that put a tickle in her stomach. Dismissing her reaction, she glanced his way and saw a giant can of stewed tomatoes and one of crushed.

He reached for several hockey-puck-sized mushrooms, his knife a blur as he chopped them into small bits.

"What are you making?"

"Spaghetti sauce."

Her eyes widened. "You make your own?"

He nodded.

"I've never known anyone who did that." She turned off the water and transferred the full pot to the counter space on her left, then began to fill the other container. "Word is you're the best cook here."

"I don't know how much that's worth coming from people who act like they haven't eaten in a month every time we sit down."

She grinned at his dry tone. "Maybe they're all bad cooks, like I am. That makes it easy to appreciate someone who's good."

Shutting off the water, she carried the full pot to the stove and switched on a large back burner. When she started to return for the other container, he passed it to her, muscles flexing up his hair-dusted forearms.

"Thanks." She set the pot on the range, then frowned. "I'm taking over the stove. Do you need one of these back burners?"

"Not for a while. One of the front ones will be okay for now."

She stepped aside as he carried over a large stockpot and placed it on the stove. He added chopped peppers and garlic.

She kept an eye on her water, watching as he poured half the can of stewed tomatoes into a restaurant-sized blender with half a can of the crushed.

Attaching the lid, he turned on the appliance. Holding out a big plastic spoon, he inclined his head toward the stove. "Can you stir the peppers and garlic for a minute?"

She glanced at the simmering paste, asking uncertainly, "Is that all? Just stir?"

He grinned, revealing deep dimples that coaxed a smile from her. "Yeah, but if you let it scorch, there'll be hell to pay with the crew."

"Can't you give me something easier? Something that won't cost my life if I screw it up?"

"There isn't anything easier," he said dryly.

"Oh." Wrinkling her nose, she took the plastic spoon from him and shifted her attention to the deep pot.

He suddenly leaned in to reach between her and the stove, turning on the oven. Jen drew in a deep breath of clean male as he straightened to move down the counter away from her.

He opened an upper cabinet, pulling out two loaves of bread. Walking behind her, he took butter and provolone cheese from the refrigerator, then returned to set the items next to the bread. He took two huge bags of uncooked spaghetti from another cabinet. "How're you doing with the sauce?"

"I don't know," she said wryly. "I'm too worried about being hurt if I mess it up."

"I'll take it from here." Looking amused, he slid the spoon from her hand and rested one hip against the edge of the counter.

He had the thickest lashes she'd ever seen on a man. She glanced over and noticed one pot of water boiling. After turning off the burner and moving the cookware to the front of the stove, she added several family-sized tea bags. She put on the lid to let the brew steep for five minutes. From the corner of her eye, she could see McClain watching her intently. Her nerves jangled.

After a moment, he moved the stockpot to the empty back burner and poured in the blended tomatoes. He reduced the heat and puréed the remaining tomatoes before adding them.

"So, what's going to happen when it's your turn to cook? You're on the schedule for the next shift."

"I like you, so I'm going to do you a favor. You should call in sick that day."

A grin tugged at his mouth, causing a little flutter in her stomach. "Didn't you cook at your old firehouse?"

"Once."

"How'd you get away with that?"

"When you taste my cooking, you'll know."

He chuckled. "You can't be that bad."

"Oh, I can. I'm more a wash-the-dishes kind of girl."

"My sister's like that." He added sugar to the sauce. "She can barely make a sandwich."

"Hey! I can make sandwiches."

"That's what she says, too."

She laughed. "Do you only have the one sister?"

"I have a brother, too. Collier." McClain measured out basil and dried oregano, which Jen recognized only because of the spice labels on the bottles. "He's one of Presley's fire investigators."

"Three of you, huh? That's nice." The old familiar mix of envy and longing stabbed through her.

He stirred the ingredients thoroughly then placed the spoon on a trivet beside the stove. "That needs to simmer about forty minutes. Do you have any siblings?"

"Nope, just me," she answered breezily. She'd been given up at birth by an unwed mother and raised by her aunt.

"How was it being an only child?"

"Okay."

Aunt Camille always felt Jen had been dumped on her after her teenage mother ran away, and her aunt was right. Jen had never been abused, had always had enough to eat and a place to sleep, but the underlying resentment from her aunt meant their relationship was mostly made up of tension.

She'd had no real family until Mark and his family. The reminder of how that had turned out still caused a crushing tightness in her chest. They had blamed her for his refusal to take his medication, which led to his permanent hospitalization. That made losing them worse than never having had a family.

After what she'd been through with her ex-fiancé, the way she'd failed him, she'd never get close to anyone in that way again.

Pushing away the painful thoughts, she searched for an impersonal topic. "This is a nice station house. How long has it been here?"

"About ten years." Walker returned to the sink and began washing the blender and other utensils he'd used. "It's one of the newer ones, built when Presley started its last growth spurt. Stations Three, Four and Five have male and female bunk rooms and bathrooms. One and Two still share everything."

"The separate locker rooms and bathrooms are nice. My firehouse in Tulsa was the oldest in the city, so we had to share restrooms and sleeping quarters. The men and women had to remember to lock the doors when taking a shower. Most of the guys didn't remember."

"I bet that got interesting sometimes." He shot a look at her. The way his voice slid over her like black silk had sensation skimming across her skin. "We've never had any problems with the coed thing here."

"That's good to know."

He rinsed the dishes and loaded them into the dishwasher. "Anyone around here play jokes on newbies?"

"Farris, and sometimes Shep."

Jen pictured both men then honed in on the one who was also a suspect in the Payback Killer murders. "I think Farris might have already played one on me."

"Yeah?" Plucking a towel from a nearby drawer, McClain dried his hands.

The savory aroma of cooking vegetables and spices filled the kitchen. Jen pulled a large copper canister marked Sugar toward her and opened it. Talking about pranks had her checking to make sure the sweetener hadn't been switched to salt. "Farris said about three years ago, a firefighter from this station house tried to kill Shelby Jessup."

"That's actually true."

"Really!" She shot him a quick look, digging through the drawer of cooking utensils. "Measuring cups?"

"They should be in there."

She pulled the drawer all the way out, then shook her head.

Dropping the towel to the counter, McClain checked the drawers on his side of the stove, but came up empty-handed. "Oh, wait. Trudeau had cleanup duty last shift. He never puts anything back where he found it. Look up here."

He stepped over next to her and opened the closest top cabinet.

The heat from his body wrapped around her, causing her throat to tighten. "I don't see them in there."

Easing behind her, he reached around to open the other cabinet. "A-ha, here they are."

When he leaned full into her to snag a stack of measuring cups, Jen froze. So did McClain.

His front was pressed into her back. Hard chest, hard belly, hard...everything, she amended, as she felt the solid line of his body all the way down hers. His heady male scent filled her head.

In that suspended moment, probably no longer than two or three seconds, his breath feathered across her neck, and adrenaline shot straight through her. She stiffened, squashing the buzz of energy.

He cleared his throat, placed the measuring cups on the counter and shut the cabinet, moving away so quickly Jen felt a brush of air.

Though her hands felt thick and clumsy, she managed to scoop out the necessary amount of sugar and dump it into the beverage dispenser. "So, what happened with Shelby?"

"One night, she walked in on a friend who'd been attacked. The attacker was about to set the woman on fire." His voice, gravelly and rough when he started, smoothed out.

"Oh, my gosh!" Jen breathed, uncovering the steeping brew and pouring the hot tea into the container. She stirred until the sugar dissolved completely. "And then?"

"The firefighter Shelby saw torching her friend shoved her over a balcony, and as a result of the fall she lost her memory."

"For how long?"

"As far as I know, she still hasn't fully remembered that

night, but the bastard didn't know she had no recall. He tried more than once to kill her in order to make sure she couldn't ID him to the cops. During one of those attempts, he lured her to a building and torched it. Every company responded to that call. He was caught red-handed. Needless to say, he's no longer a firefighter. Now he's in the pen at McAlester."

"Is Shelby okay? Did she suffer any other side effects from the trauma?"

"She hasn't appeared to."

"That's lucky. The whole thing sounds awful." What Jen really wanted to know was about the tragedy McClain had suffered. She wanted to hear it in his own words. Wanted to know how it had affected him. If he was dealing with it by taking revenge on scum who were just like the brutal mugger who'd killed his wife and unborn child. Of course, she couldn't ask that. "So have you always lived in Presley?"

"Yeah."

"And worked out of Station Three?"

"No."

"When did you transfer to this station house?"

Crossing his arms, he gave her a steady, inscrutable look. "You always ask this many questions?"

"Is that privileged information?" she teased.

Tension coiled through his body and his jaw locked.

Shoot, she'd hoped they were past that.

After a short pause, he said, "I've always lived in Presley. I came to Station Three about two and a half years ago."

Around the time of his wife's death. Was that why his voice suddenly turned flat, his eyes remote?

She started to ask if he regretted the transfer, then decided to back off. She couldn't press, not yet anyway. "That sauce smells wonderful."

After filling the dispenser of sweetened tea with cold water, she removed the second pot from the burner and added tea bags.

Walker began heating water for the pasta, and Jen stored the two prepared containers in the fridge.

She exhaled slowly. What was it about Walker McClain that got to her so fast? Made her want to know things about him that had nothing to do with these four murders?

That kind of curiosity was dangerous. Stupid. She had to stay focused on her investigation of him.

McClain was, hands down, the sexiest, most affecting suspect she'd ever been assigned to, and her gut told her he would also be the toughest to get close to.

To accomplish that she would have to get him to drop his guard. Without dropping her own.

Walker didn't know what the hell had happened with Lawson in the kitchen, but he didn't like it. It had been unexpected. And unnerving.

Three hours later, his blood was still running hot. He'd done just fine living in a vacuum that consisted of work and trying to find Holly's killer. He wanted to keep living there.

He liked women. He dated, but he hadn't felt such a sharp awareness of another woman since his wife. He was still irritated that his brain had gone to neutral when he'd seen Lawson's incredibly blue eyes, but when he'd felt her, breathed in her musky floral scent, his body had gone hard all over. His hormones felt like they were in overdrive.

Well, why wouldn't they be? he asked himself. He hadn't slept with a woman in two and a half years, and Jen Lawson was gorgeous. Smelled like this side of heaven. Her scent was different. Refreshing. Or it would've been if it hadn't settled in his lungs and stayed there. Even surrounded by sweating firefighters and smoke, Walker knew he'd be able to track her.

But that only proved he wasn't dead, regardless of feeling that way until the day before yesterday, when she'd shown up. Everything about her had shocked his senses back to life. That had to be why he was still thinking about it.

And he was done, he decided, as the rescue truck sped to a call to "assist a party."

He turned his thoughts to his day off yesterday. He had visited the local pawnshops, as he did every two weeks. There was still no sign of the gold necklace that had been stolen from his wife when she'd been beaten to death. Made of entwined H's, Walker had given Holly the distinctive chain after her pregnancy caused her fingers to swell and she couldn't wear her wedding ring. After all this time, he knew it was a long shot to keep searching for the jewelry, but he would.

Lawson sat in the jump seat facing his as the truck raced to the address they'd been given. She talked and joked with Shelby, Farris and Shep. Walker joined in occasionally.

The vehicle rolled to a stop in front of a small redbrick house with a neatly tended yard. He grabbed his medic kit, aware that Lawson jumped out right behind him.

A slight gray-haired woman stood in the door, waiting for them, tears streaming down her face.

"She's in the bathroom. Through that door!" The woman gestured wildly toward a bedroom with a quilt-topped bed.

"What's your name, ma'am?" Walker said as he hurried past her.

"Sue. My sister is Carol. Carol Allen."

"It's going to be all right, Sue," Lawson soothed.

"I tried not to move her," the woman said. "But I put a robe on her. She would kill me if I let anyone see her in the bathtub."

Walker approached the bathroom, thankful for Shelby and Farris providing a distraction by asking the patient's sister what had happened. He moved into the room with Lawson close behind. So close her scent whispered around him.

Annoyed, his voice was a little brusque. "Mrs. Allen? Fire Department."

"Yes!" the woman responded in a labored voice. "Thank goodness you're here. Is my sister all right?"

"She is. She's worried about you." The water had been drained out, and the patient was covered with a thick terrycloth robe. The woman weighed at least twice as much as her sister, which explained why the slightly built Sue hadn't been able to help.

The bathroom was tiny. The green-and-white-tiled space was nearly swallowed up by a huge claw-foot tub against the wall. There was barely enough room for him and Lawson between the tub and a white pedestal sink.

Pulling on his latex gloves, Walker knelt near the patient's head. "Are you hurt anywhere, ma'am?"

"I think I broke something."

"Where does it hurt?"

"My lower back and tailbone. I can't get out of here."

His initial assessment revealed no blood or wounds on the pale, trembling woman. "Has this happened before, Mrs. Allen?"

"No, thank goodness. Can you imagine? I was trying to get out of the tub, and I slipped and fell right on my hind end."

Walker bit back a smile at her phrasing and noticed Jen did, too. "My partner is going to assess you for other injuries while I check your pulse and blood pressure."

Carol Allen seemed calm. The situation was non-life-threatening, and Walker determined her earlier labored breathing was the result of panic rather than a respiratory problem.

He and Lawson were fully trained paramedics, but the other firefighters were basic EMTs. The full-time paramedics were en route to the scene and would take over once they arrived.

As Lawson slipped on her gloves and went to her knees beside him, she smiled at the older woman. "Let me know if anything hurts when I touch it."

"All right."

As she began searching for other injuries starting at the patient's hips, Lawson's arm brushed Walker's.

Muscles tensing, he fixed his thoughts on the patient. Her pulse was slightly accelerated, her eyes alert.

After a few moments, Lawson glanced over at him. "No pain anywhere else."

He smiled at Mrs. Allen. "The paramedics will be here soon. In the meantime, we need to get some information from you."

As Jen jotted down the patient's name, age, any allergies and medications, Walker tried to figure out the best way to get Mrs. Allen out of the tub. He decided the best course would be to put one foot inside the claw-foot tub and straddle the other side. Once in position, the heavy woman could be lifted by her armpits.

Walker adjusted his gloves. Even though the patient wasn't panicked, she was in an embarrassing position. To put her at ease, he squeezed her shoulder. "What is that great smell coming from your kitchen?"

"Gingersnaps."

"Homemade?"

"Is there any other kind?"

He grinned. "Not where I come from. That's what I make, too."

"How did you learn that—" her gaze went to the name embroidered on his uniform shirt "—Mr. McClain?"

"Walker," he offered, as Jen shifted beside him. "I learned to cook from my grandmother."

Lawson twisted toward him and placed her clipboard behind them on the floor. He eased back, unable to pull his gaze from the sweet line of her neck.

It took half a second for his brain to engage, which added to his earlier aggravation. Hell, where was the ambulance? The paramedics?

Finally, he heard the sirens announcing their arrival. Relief rolled through him when, a few seconds later, a female paramedic appeared in the doorway. She grimaced. "Sorry it took so long. Dispatch gave us the wrong street name."

Walker nodded, bringing the trim blonde up to date on the situation. He told her his plan for getting the patient out of the tub.

She gave him a warm smile. "That's good. Can you and your partner get Mrs. Allen out on your own?"

"Yeah."

"Since you guys are already in position, we'll roll the cot inside and you can move her. We'll take over once you have her settled."

Walker nodded. "Mrs. Allen, I need for you to be very still while Lawson and I lift you out then put you on the stretcher."

"All right."

The woman's voice was calm, but he registered concern in her eyes. He moved behind her to the head of the tub as she asked, "Did your grandmother teach you to make anything besides gingersnaps?"

"He whips up a killer pasta sauce," Jen volunteered with a smile.

Once the stretcher was laid flat next to the old-fashioned tub, Walker put his left foot inside it and straddled the other side. He shifted a couple of times, trying to find the most stable footing. The cast-iron edge of the tub dug into his inner thigh.

"Pasta sauce?" the older woman repeated. "Do you use wine in it?"

"No, but I'll have to try that. Ma'am, I'm going to slide my arms under yours."

"Okay." The older woman flattened her arms along her sides, securing the robe that draped her. "I'm ready."

Walker nodded at Lawson and she moved to the foot of the tub, wrapping her hands around Mrs. Allen's ankles. "Mrs. Allen, after we settle you on the cot, we'll place you on your side to relieve any pressure on your tailbone."

"Okay."

He slipped his forearms beneath the woman's arms then readjusted his stance slightly.

"What about you, Ms. Lawson?" the patient asked. "What's your speciality?"

"Sweet tea, and that's about it." She held Mrs. Allen's legs steady as Walker lifted her.

As soon as he raised the woman about a foot, Lawson re-arranged her hold to provide more support for the woman's lower back.

The muscles in Walker's arms and shoulders burned as he slowly moved the patient.

She winced, but kept her gaze on his partner. "Did you learn to make sweet tea from your grandmother, dear?"

Walker heard the stress beneath the woman's words and understood she was trying to focus on something besides the pain.

"No, ma'am. I never knew my grandparents."

"What a pity," Mrs. Allen murmured.

Lawson shifted enough to allow Walker to step out of the

tub. As they slowly lowered the woman to the stretcher, he flicked a glance at Jen. No grandparents. No siblings. What was her story?

"You're doing great, Mrs. Allen," he said, wondering if his new coworker had any family at all.

He shoved away his curiosity about her background. It was none of his business and, more important, had nothing to do with this call. As Walker gently settled Mrs. Allen on her side, Lawson draped a blanket over her.

She reached up to draw it over the patient's shoulders at the same time Walker leaned forward to carefully buckle a strap across her middle. His temple grazed Jen's.

"Sorry," she said quietly, shifting back.

One more millimeter and he could've touched his lips to her silky cheek.

Hell! He wanted about twenty feet of space between him and Lawson, but Mrs. Allen was the only person who was important. It didn't matter that his partner's arousing scent was going to his head. And other body parts.

The desire brought a flash of guilt. There was only one woman for him, and she was dead.

Walker wanted out of here, away from Lawson, but he tried to curb his impatience.

Lawson rose. "Mrs. Allen, we're going to turn you over to the paramedics now. They'll take good care of you."

"Thank you, dear."

"You're welcome." She retrieved her kit and left the room.

Still kneeling next to the patient, Walker patted her shoulder. "You're in good hands, Mrs. Allen."

"Thank you, Walker. Thank you very much."

"I'm going to try your suggestion in my pasta sauce."

"You'll like it."

Smiling, he picked up his kit and left the patient with the paramedics. Once in the living room, he found Sue offering a plate of gingersnaps to Lawson, Jessup and Farris.

The little woman tottered to him. "Cookie?"

"Thanks." Taking one, he bit into the soft, spiced sweet.

"These are a lot better than yours, McClain," Farris ribbed.

"Yeah," Jessup joined in. "Yours always taste like dirt."

He waved off their teasing and said goodbye to the older woman, starting toward the door. Sue surprised him by suddenly wrapping her arms around his waist and hugging him tight.

It was automatic to hug her in return.

"Thank you. I know this was probably silly to all of you." Tears filled her eyes. "But I don't know what we would've done if you hadn't come."

"We were happy to help."

Over the woman's head, Lawson's sapphire eyes met his and she smiled. That smile had something hot and sharp pushing up under Walker's ribs.

He jerked his gaze from hers and released Sue. After a round of goodbyes, the others followed him to the door. Once outside, he breathed his first full breath since getting in the rescue truck with Jen Lawson.

She was the last one out, but it didn't matter. Walker felt her as if she were walking beside him. Whatever the hell was going on with him, it had to stop. Now.

He had to work with Jen Lawson, but he didn't have to let her get to him. And he wouldn't.

Chapter 3

Hours later, her stomach still fluttery, Jen admitted she was more aware than she liked of Walker McClain. Curious about things that didn't have anything to do with the investigation, which was all she should think about.

So…she wasn't going to let him affect her in any other way. There was no reason he ever had to know she'd been so conscious of him.

Nearly an hour ago, she'd come to her bunk trying to catch some sleep like the others before their next call. It wasn't going to happen. Her nerves were shimmering and she was wound up tighter than the chain on a saw.

Knowing she wouldn't be getting sleep anytime soon, Jen got up. Moonlight glowed through the thick blinds on the windows over the bunks. Careful not to wake Shelby, Jen pulled on a pair of gray knit shorts and a sports bra under her baggy PFD T-shirt in case they were called out. Maybe she could watch TV. Or find something to read. She opened the door as quietly as possible, stepping into the hallway illuminated dimly by a light from the kitchen downstairs.

The door of the men's bunk room was slightly ajar. And from the corner of her eye, Jen caught a movement near the metal staircase. A shadow, male.

Moving the few yards to the railing, she got there in time to identify McClain. Her heart tripped. Maybe he was out of bed for the same reason she was, in which case it wouldn't matter if they saw each other. But instinct had her wait until he disappeared from view before she crept down the stairs.

Once on the ground floor, a quick glance into the kitchen told her he wasn't there. Or in the captain's darkened office at the rear of the bay. The spicy aroma of pasta sauce still lingered, underlaid by the bite of engine oil.

All the bay's doors were closed. Where had McClain gone? To her right was a regular exit door leading out the side of the firehouse. She silently opened it and peered around the steel frame. Seeing no one, she slipped out.

Cool night air flowed around her, causing a quick rise of gooseflesh on her arms. Careful to stay flattened against the brick wall, she eased along the side of the firehouse and peeked around the corner.

Tuning out the chirp of insects, she scanned the four-lane road. The tang of fuel rose from the street as an occasional car drove past. Beneath that, she could smell fresh-cut grass coming from the large pasture across from the firehouse. Her gaze shifted to the Helping Hands shelter, and there he was.

He stood under a streetlight talking to a disheveled man. A duffel bag sat at the stranger's feet, probably holding all he had in the world.

McClain spoke to the man intently for a couple of minutes, and the man shook his head several times. Frustration clawed through her. How was she supposed to find out what he was up to? Besides a few widely spaced trees, there was no cover between here and Helping Hands. If she stepped away from the fire station to overhear his conversation, she'd be in plain sight.

The unfamiliar man picked up his bag and hefted it over his shoulder. The discussion appeared to be ending.

She ducked behind the corner of the firehouse and hurried back inside, careful to be quiet. She quickly made it to the kitchen, expecting to hear McClain any second, but she didn't.

She could've gone on upstairs, but she wanted to wait. See how long it took him to return. See if he *did* return. And if she noticed anything different about him when he did.

Why had he been talking to the man outside the homeless shelter? Why was it taking him so long to return to the firehouse? Where *was* he?

After a few minutes, Jen considered going back outside and trying to find him. She had more questions in the investigation, no answers. Nothing to report, other than the man was a good cook. And he smelled wonderful. But she wasn't concerned yet for failing to learn anything new about McClain or the recent murder victims. Operations like this took months, sometimes years. People had to come to trust her, accept her. That wouldn't happen in three days.

Meanwhile, she had to be aware of McClain's every move. Unfortunately, that wasn't a problem. She was aware of him in ways that had nothing to do with him being a suspect.

The man she'd observed today during the tub rescue didn't seem like a cold-blooded killer to Jen. There was nothing cold about him. After they had all left the scene, she had waited for him to make some joke about the situation.

Other firefighters would have. Even she might have. But the only comment he'd made was "nice ladies."

He'd been gentle and sweet to both women, even when the one had startled him with a full-body hug. Jen found that appealing on a whole other level. He was very good at his job. In that regard she had no qualms about partnering up with him for fires, rescues or SWAT calls.

As to the physical awareness, she would box that up in a separate part of her mind just as she'd learned to do with her emotions regarding Mark. And with her last undercover job, when she'd become too close to one of the girls implicated in the sex ring at the firehouse. That reminder helped firm her resolve.

She didn't see how a man with such kindness in his eyes could be a murderer, but she had no evidence to support that opinion. There was nothing to prove he was the Payback Killer. And there was nothing to prove he wasn't, she reminded herself sternly.

When she finally heard the door open, the clock showed he'd been gone almost twenty-five minutes.

Scurrying to the refrigerator, she had it open and was looking inside when McClain's voice rumbled behind her.

"What are you doing?"

Starting, she turned to see him in the doorway, his handsome features drawn, his jaw covered with dark stubble. The smudges beneath his green eyes tugged at her. He looked agitated, but not as though he had murdered someone.

Pasting a sheepish expression on her face, she filched a peanut butter cup from a bag in the fridge and held up the candy. "I couldn't sleep, so I thought I'd scrounge for something to eat. Want one?"

"No thanks." His gaze trailed over her, lingering on her breasts then moving down to her legs.

His eyes darkened, and that look sizzled across her skin. Every nerve ending tingled. When he turned away, she tried to keep him talking.

"I didn't wake you, did I? I tried to be quiet."

"You didn't wake me."

She smiled. "You couldn't sleep, either?"

Instead of answering her, he started for the stairs. "Think I'll try to get some."

"Good night." She mentally ground her teeth. Getting anywhere with this guy was like trying to breach a fort.

"Night."

She padded quietly to the kitchen door in time to see him step onto the second-floor landing and turn the corner. He sure wasn't a hardship to look at, especially from the back.

Remembering the flash of heat in his heavy-lidded gaze moments ago had her scrambling to adjust her thoughts. She had to keep her focus on Walker McClain the suspect, not Walker McClain the man.

His late-night meeting in front of the shelter was something new to report to the fire marshal and the detectives working this case, but it wasn't much. She told herself her dissatisfaction was caused by the minuscule amount of information she had, not because she was starting to like Walker McClain.

Last night had been one of Walker's worst in a while. First, his questions to the homeless shelter's two new arrivals had yielded the same answers they did every time he asked. Neither person knew nor had seen a man with a knife scar across the knuckles of his right hand.

Then Walker had returned to the firehouse and come across Jen Lawson. He'd already been frustrated, and seeing her had shoved that frustration over into something hot and reckless.

He hadn't been able to stop looking at her. All of her. Especially her sleek, bare legs. And that pissed him off.

He'd worked with plenty of women, had never had a problem looking past the physical to how they did their jobs. And he resented having a problem doing it with Jen Lawson.

As he'd gone up to the bunk room, he wondered how long she'd been in the kitchen, how long she might stay there. Then he forced himself to stop thinking about her and hit the mattress.

He'd fallen asleep almost immediately and woken up less than an hour later, drenched in sweat, murmuring Holly's name. The dream had taken him back to the night of her murder. Him riding in the ambulance with her, knowing it was too late even before she was pronounced by a doctor who'd tried everything to save her and their unborn child. If he hadn't bought that damn necklace for her, she'd probably still be alive.

The memories always sucked him in like quicksand. On the days after he had the nightmare, he didn't like being around anyone except his family, and sometimes not even them. He didn't want to see people today, let alone Jen Lawson. But he—they—had SWAT training. There was no getting out of it.

At one o'clock that afternoon, he pulled up behind the training center complex. Buildings for administration, classroom space, vehicle storage and maintenance took up the front half of the thirty-seven-acre property. The drill tower, driving course and houses used for practicing various procedures sat a couple of hundred yards away from the main facilities.

Because of their vests, Walker could identify the SWAT team on the rise ahead, and he got out of his SUV to join them. He grabbed his vest and helmet, rounded the building's corner and started up the hill.

As he neared, he could see Lawson was already there, talking to Troy Inman, the team commander. It only then occurred to Walker that he hadn't asked her if she knew how to get here. Poor manners and poor teamwork on his part.

She and the sinewy, sandy-haired SWAT leader stood beside the drill tower, where firefighters practiced cutting holes in roofs, tearing out walls and carrying human-sized dummies down flights of stairs, among other things.

Inman laughed at something she said, then squeezed her shoulder. Walker was surprised by a flash of irritation. His longtime friend acted as if he were well-acquainted with Lawson.

The SWAT medics from Presley's other four firehouses stood a short distance away in a loose circle. Next to Inman's lean, six-foot frame, Jen appeared small. Her hair was neatly braided, and her helmet was tucked under her left arm. She, like all members of the SWAT team, wore a ballistic vest supplied by Presley PD.

Those for the firefighter/paramedics were marked front and back with Medic in bold white letters. Her blow-out pack, with all the necessary medical supplies, was in a pouch on her vest. Every officer wore it in the same location, and each one had it at all times during a call. The supplies in their pouch were to be used on them if they were injured.

As Walker moved in her direction, he greeted everyone.

Inman glanced over his shoulder. "Hey, man."

"Hey." Walker shook his friend's hand as Lawson gave him a small smile. In the bright light, her eyes were flame blue.

"I was just catching up with your new partner," the SWAT leader said.

Walker had known Inman for years. Holly and the commander's wife—ex-wife—had been good friends. Now Holly was dead and Inman's ex-wife had moved away a year ago. "Catching up?"

"We met a couple of years ago at a medic training seminar," Lawson said in her husky velvet voice, her eyes smiling into his.

As happened every time, Walker was fascinated by their vibrant, intense shade. His train of thought skipped off track for a half second. Was that color real or did she wear tinted contacts?

He felt as though her gaze could laser right through him. He was glad when she put on her sunglasses.

As the other team members joined them, Walker eased into the space next to Jen. "I guess you found the place all right?"

"Yes. I had good directions."

He thought he detected a trace of nerves in her voice. Maybe she was anxious about her first team exercise.

Inman introduced her to the others, then looked down at the clipboard he held. "We're working in two-medic units today, with your usual partner. Your job is to locate the casualty, conduct tactical combat care if necessary and evacuate the wounded to the van."

He turned, facing the five-acre tract at the bottom of the hill opposite the drill tower, simulated to look like a neighborhood street. "We'll stage at the end of the block and use the training house that's normally reserved for gas mask drills. I want your MTAs before we get started."

The medical threat assessment was a rescue plan that considered factors impacting the team—individual medical history, environment, fatigue, nutrition, potential threats. It also included a strategy to extricate and transport patients.

The team's health information could be gathered prior to or during a mission. Walker had what he needed for everyone except Jen, but it didn't take long to get her medical history and background.

After she answered his questions, Walker noticed her studying a map. She glanced up. "Thought I'd better start figuring out where things are around here."

"Have any questions about Presley or anything?"

"Not yet."

He nodded, his thoughts returning to his MTA. Checking the area, he noted the closest cover where they could take victims, as well as the extraction point and rallying location for regrouping.

Inman motioned everyone in closer. "Today, the medics' primary job is tactical medicine. McClain, your secondary responsibility is breacher. Lawson, you're driving the van."

Both positions were good roles for a SWAT medic. The breacher staged at the point of entry and the driver was able to follow the team in without any delay.

Inman assigned one medic to be ready with a fire extinguisher, another as "cuffer" to assist the police with handcuffing if needed. The SWAT team would provide security at the front and rear of the house.

Once everyone knew their post, they studied the drawing of the house's floor plan that Inman had flattened against the side of the van. Lawson slid behind the wheel of the vehicle as everyone loaded up, then she drove to the staging area.

Once there, she stood beside Walker, her attention on Inman.

"The building needs to be searched," he said. "The windows are blacked out and light is not an option for anyone, including the medics. Not a flashlight, not a penlight, not a laser pointer. Even if you need to treat someone."

Jen leaned toward Walker, her voice low. "Is that because of the Israeli tactical doctors who were killed trying to treat a patient in a firing zone? What was it they used? A laryngoscope?"

He nodded, his gaze caught by a strand of dark hair blowing across her dewy skin. The light from the small fiber-optic instrument used to look in the patient's throat had been enough for a sniper to sight his targets and fire two fatal shots.

That incident, among others, had inspired the concept of SWAT medics. It made sense. The medics were already on location. Putting them on the tactical team allowed them to provide immediate care without having to wait for police to clear a scene. Presley's fire and police departments had worked in tandem from the beginning to establish the program. The city had recently joined the growing number of departments across the country that allowed their medics to carry a weapon on tactical calls.

Inman glanced at Walker and Jen. "You'll go in one team at a time and I'm clocking you. McClain and Lawson, medic up!"

They waited as the tactical team searched the house then positioned themselves at the front and rear of the residence.

After they gave the all clear, Walker took the lead, glancing behind him. Jen nodded to tell him she was in sync with him. From here on, until the patient was out of the hot zone, there would be no talking, no noise.

Once inside the small house, they were swallowed up by thick darkness. The air was stuffy. Not one speck of light got through the blacked-out windows or around the door frames. Walker went to his belly and crawled along the floor, with Lawson close behind doing the same. He bumped into a foot and stopped. Jen halted, too.

While they'd waited for the search, he and Jen had agreed

each would examine one side of any patient they found. Walker began his check and felt Jen move to do the same. Her surgical-gloved hand touched his to let him know she was doing as they'd discussed.

Walker felt his way up the victim's body, determined the person was male and found a bleeding leg wound on the man's upper left thigh. Because Walker and Jen were in such close quarters, he could feel her body heat. And without smoke, nothing masked her tantalizing scent. That soft floral-and-woman smell could easily distract him if he let it, but he wouldn't. Walker set his jaw and focused on his job.

Though completely enclosed in darkness, he had no problem finding Jen to tap two of his fingers against her hand in the signal they'd agreed meant yes. There was injury on his side.

She responded with one tap, telling him there were no wounds on her side. Their job was to treat and move, so Walker got busy. The patient had no trouble with his breathing, so there was no need to keep his airway open. Walker pressed Jen's hand firmly to the victim's wound then took a CAT tourniquet from his blow-out pack.

Her head was close to his as he applied the combat application tourniquet. The whisper of her breath against his cheek had his brain fighting off an image of her breathing against him in the dark for another reason entirely. Was it getting hotter in here? He was hotter.

As they worked, Lawson moved her hand precisely when he needed it, applied and released pressure without any prompting from him. It was almost as if her actions mirrored his thoughts. They found a steady brisk rhythm, their movements in perfect sync.

Satisfied the blood flow was slowed, Walker tapped

Jen's hand twice to indicate they were ready to transport. With her going to the patient's feet and Walker remaining at the man's head, they began moving the victim, still careful to be silent.

Once outside the house, it took Walker's eyes a few seconds to adjust to the glaring sunlight. They were covered by SWAT as they transferred the patient into the van. During the simulated ten-minute ride to Presley Regional Medical Center, he and Jen concentrated on preventing more blood loss. She was with him every step of the way.

He had thought Pickett was his best partner, but after Lawson's performance today, Walker was considering changing his mind.

He admired the way she sized up a situation quickly, didn't waste time or motion. Once he'd gotten past the heat of her body teasing his, they'd operated like a well-oiled machine. For those few moments, they hadn't been a man and a woman. Just two medics doing their job as though they'd always worked together. Walker decided he wouldn't mind teaming with her.

After the patient was delivered to the "hospital," Jen and Walker climbed out of the van to a smattering of applause from the group.

She gave a puzzled smile.

Inman grinned. "McClain, you and Lawson beat your best time with Pickett by almost a minute."

Pleased and surprised, Walker glanced at Jen. "Good job."

"You, too."

After their routine debriefing, they stayed until all the teams had finished. She said goodbye shortly after the commander dismissed them.

Inman's gaze tracked her as she moved down the rise toward the back of the training center where she'd parked. He glanced at Walker. "So, what did you think?"

"She's good. Really good."

"Some woman actually impressed you?"

"Yes." He shrugged. "I wasn't sure how we would work together."

His friend grinned. "Thought about doing anything with her besides working?"

"Hell, no." Walker's response was pure reflex. And a lie.

"Twenty bucks says you will."

He grunted. Just because he'd thought about it once—or twice—didn't mean he would do it again.

After confirming he would meet Inman later at the ball-park for their softball game against a team of Oklahoma City firefighters, Walker started for his car.

In the close confines of the dark house, it would've been easy to let Lawson get to him, but he hadn't. Guilt nudged at him anyway. He loved his wife, and even though she'd been gone two and a half years, it didn't sit well that he was so strongly attracted to another woman. But attraction didn't mean he wanted to take action.

Carrying his helmet under his arm, he stripped off his vest and tucked it there, too. He strode down the side of the training center. Despite the comfortable temperature today, he was sweating beneath the helmet and his Kevlar vest like everyone else. His T-shirt was plastered to him, soaked. He always brought extras so he could change.

Reaching back to grab a handful of shirt, he pulled it over his head, swiping it across his slick chest as he rounded the corner. And froze.

Sweet Mother—

Lawson was straight ahead, next to her Jeep Wrangler. She'd peeled off her dark PFD T-shirt and now wore a snug white tank top. She was bent over, and for one split second he thought her lush breasts might overflow that shirt. What the hell was she doing?

He noted absently that her SWAT boots sat next to her red vehicle, and he finally registered she was putting on a pair of tennis shoes. With each movement, her upper arms pressed her breasts together, plumping them up even more.

Everything around him faded and he was aware only of the dark throb of need in his blood. The faint sheen of perspiration in her cleavage had him wanting to lick her. Peel that tank top down and touch her bare flesh.

Then she straightened and saw him. "Oh, hi."

"Hey." His throat was tight, as was the rest of his body.

The white cotton top was slightly damp from her bra, and Walker could see the perfect shape of her breasts. When her nipples tightened, his chest caved in, and every inch of his body went hard. He was absurdly, illogically, glad none of the other guys were around.

The smile on her face dimmed as her gaze slid over his chest. For one unguarded moment, he saw a flash of the same raw, undisguised hunger slamming through his body.

What was wrong with him? It was like his whole system had short-circuited. *Say something, you idiot,* he thought. Gripping his T-shirt so hard his palm burned, he shook himself out of his stupor. "I thought you were already gone."

"About to be." A flush stained her cheeks, worked its way to her chest as her gaze skittered away. She pointed at the wadded-up T-shirt in the front passenger seat. "I had to get out of that. It was soaked."

"Yeah, mine too." He held up his own garment, amazed his voice sounded steady.

"Where you headed?"

"Home for a shower."

She groaned, slicking the back of her hand across her forehead. "I'm meeting a friend to go running. A shower sounds really good."

An image flashed of her naked, water streaming over her breasts, down her flat belly. Walker slammed the door on that mental picture. He didn't want to think about her in the shower. Or anywhere else.

She tossed her boots into the backseat of her Wrangler. "See ya at tomorrow's training session."

"See ya." He stood beside his SUV, trying to get his bearings as she drove off. When his brain started working again, he let out a curse.

Had he actually believed he could think of Jen as just his partner? Believed he wasn't all *that* affected by her?

After what he'd just seen, there was no way he could deny wanting her. The hard pulsing of his body had him imagining all kinds of things he wanted to do to her, with her.

He'd said he wouldn't let her get to him, but she'd gotten to him, all right. Every damn inch of him.

Chapter 4

All Walker had done was look, but Jen's skin tingled as though he had dragged his hands all over her body.

Even three days after their first SWAT exercise, she was trying to shut out that scorching moment between them. Trying to dodge the image branded in her brain of that granite-hard chest, the sweep of dark hair from his pecs to his flat belly.

She could not want her chief suspect. So during their scheduled physical fitness time late in the afternoon, she'd come to the workout room in the firehouse to sweat out her frustration. Too bad her kickboxing couldn't help her sweat out this nerve-racking attraction.

Today was the first day of their next four-day shift and she'd seen him this morning during roll call. Ever since, her nerves had shimmered with awareness.

She tried to combat that by thinking about her latest

covert visit with the fire marshal and the detectives. She'd told them about Walker's speaking with the man in front of the homeless shelter, then told them how long it had taken him to return to the firehouse. Observations like that were all she'd scored so far, and the cops couldn't do much with it. She had even less on Farris at this point.

After several minutes of jabbing and punching at the weighted target, Jen's palms were wet beneath her hand-wraps, and her fitted tank top was damp. She grabbed a towel, dragging it over her face and neck. Just like that, she flashed back to the other day when Walker's gaze had done a slow glide down her body. That led to the image seared into her brain of his sweat-slick chest. She'd wanted to run her hands over his shoulders, down his torso then back up. Heat flashed across her skin. This work*out* was only getting her worked *up*.

She was almost glad when Brett Farris walked in. He wore tennis shoes and dark shorts without a shirt. His golden hair-dusted chest was nice, but her pulse didn't spike. And she wasn't tempted in the least to touch it or feel it against hers. Dang Walker McClain!

Farris headed straight for her corner. "Hey, Lawson."

"Hello." Why wasn't he wearing a shirt? She got the sense that he would have liked it if she acted as though she noticed, so she wouldn't. She focused on the upright padded target in front of her.

The muscled-up firefighter walked to the rowing machine a few feet away and added more weight, then eased down into the seat and grabbed the handlebar. Using long pulls, he began rowing. She could feel his gaze sliding over her pale blue tank and matching shorts, and thought about giving him her death glare.

"I noticed you looking under the hood of your Jeep when you got here this morning. Having car problems?"

"Oh, the stupid thing took forever to start. I was checking to see if the battery needed water."

Farris nodded. "If you ever need a ride to work, give me a call."

"All right. Thanks," she murmured. Not.

"How are you liking it here?"

"I like it a lot." She landed a hard kick to the target. Her heart rate was getting up now, helping to muffle the buzz that had been zipping through her body since seeing Walker first thing that morning.

"And the SWAT team? That's going okay, too?"

"Yes. It's a good team. Really sharp."

Farris grunted, his biceps and calf muscles bulging as he worked his upper and lower body at the rowing machine. "Are you getting along with McClain?"

She shot a look at him. "Is there some reason why we wouldn't get along?"

"He can be intense sometimes. Dark." The other man shrugged. "You know about his wife's murder, right? It still gets to him."

And Jen's job was to find out just how much. Was the un-solved murder of McClain's wife getting to him enough to become the Payback Killer? Or was there something in Farris's past that might turn him vigilante?

"They've never caught the person who did it," Farris offered.

"Do the police even have any leads?"

"No," he answered. "That scumbag is probably walking around free as a bird. Maybe the Payback Killer will catch up with him."

"And murder him?"

He shrugged. "It would be a service to society. I doubt too many people would lose sleep over it, especially McClain."

How serious was Farris? Serious enough to kill Holly McClain's murderer if the scumbag were ever found?

"Sounds like you don't have a problem with McClain. That's good."

Jen had a problem with him, all right, but it was *her* problem. An attraction problem.

"You having trouble, Lawson?" Shepherd asked cheerfully, as he came into the room along with Walker. "With whom?"

"Nobody." Jen looked at Walker and nearly choked on the word.

Oh, boy. A black T-shirt with the sleeves ripped out showed off bronze, steel-hard biceps, and the loose fabric did nothing to disguise just how defined and sculpted his chest was beneath. A chest Jen had been trying to forget.

Well, great.

At the door, he hesitated as though debating whether he wanted to come inside. Then he moved toward the opposite corner and took down a jump rope that hung over the chin-up bar. "Hey."

"Hi." She felt so shaky, she was amazed her voice worked. Grabbing her water bottle from a spot behind her, she took a long swallow.

Farris paused in his rowing strokes. "McClain, I was just asking Lawson if you were being a pain in the butt."

Jen frowned and started to protest.

Walker glanced at her. "And she said?"

"*She* said no." Jen gave them both an irritated look as she set her water down. "Hello, I'm right here."

Shep made his way to the chin-up bar in the corner, looking thoughtfully from Walker to Lawson. Farris finished at the rowing machine and moved to the back wall, picking up a couple of heavy free weights from the set stored there. Jen narrowed her focus to the kickboxing target in front of her, determined to keep from paying too much attention to McClain, but it was hard. The man was wicked gorgeous, and his presence pulsed some sort of crazy electricity through her veins.

Dylan Shepherd was plenty good-looking himself, and Farris was fine if you went for the Brad-Pitt-on-steroids type, but neither of them fired her up. Why Walker? What was it about him? And why now? Of all the times for her sex drive to wake up, this was the worst.

Walker began jumping rope, the muscles in his arms flexing with each rotation. The lean, strong legs bared by gray cotton-knit shorts clenched in sharp definition.

Farris moved behind her, close enough that Jen could feel him. "So what do you do when you aren't on duty, Lawson?"

She felt as though she was always on duty. "What do *you* do?"

He stepped up beside her, grinning. "Why don't you go out with me tomorrow and find out?"

She ignored the question, aware of the rhythmic slap of Walker's rope against the hard floor. "I heard you volunteer a lot at the homeless shelter near here."

"Yeah, but we could do something more fun than that. Something for just the two of us." He reached out and tugged lightly on her ponytail.

Want to lose that hand? she thought. Leveling a look on him, she stepped away and directed the conversation back to trying to find out about his activities. "How long have you volunteered?"

"A couple of years." He moved away with a slight frown.

Jen weighed his expression. Was he frowning because he was getting the message she wasn't interested in him? Or was it because he didn't want her asking about his volunteer work? "How did you get involved with that?"

"My church."

She arched a brow. "You don't seem like the church type."

"If you'd spend some time with me, you might find out differently."

"Or you could just answer my question," she said sweetly, aware of Walker and Shep glancing over. "I don't know much about homeless shelters. Do the people always stay at the same one? Or do they move from shelter to shelter?"

"Depends. A lot of them will stay gone during the day, panhandling on the street, then come back at night for a meal and a bed. Some of them are just passing through."

"Are they mainly people who don't want to work?"

"Some are. A lot of them are so beat up from life they just can't climb out of their pit."

"Sounds sad."

"Sometimes it is." For a moment, Farris sounded as if he actually cared, then his voice hardened. "And sometimes they're like the scum who are being murdered. Out of prison after having served their time for committing a violent crime. Going on to commit more. It's hard to want to help people like that."

"How do you know who's good and who isn't?"

"I talk to them. You'd be surprised what people will tell you. Plus the parole officers check in with the shelters. They give the director information on who's been released from prison and who's checked in with their PO."

So, Farris wouldn't have any trouble finding out who was a recently released violent offender.

"I can take you over to Helping Hands, introduce you to the director. You can go with me the next time I volunteer."

Jen considered it, but she could talk to the director on her own. If there was anything to be learned about Farris, she would get further without him. Besides, he was already hard enough to shake; she didn't need to encourage him.

"Sounds like a fun date," Shep said dryly.

"Shut up, Shepherd. Lawson, we could go do something—" Farris's gaze dropped to her chest and stayed there "—else."

"Hey, buddy!" Jen snapped her fingers to pull his attention back to her face.

From across the room, Shep laughed. "Ain't gonna happen, man."

Farris ignored the other firefighter and leaned in close, saying in a low voice, "I can be patient."

She nearly punched him instead of her kickboxing target. "Doesn't Presley have a policy against coworkers dating?"

"No."

"Really? I'm surprised. They should."

"You should go out with me," Farris wheedled. "You'd like it."

"Give it up." She shook her head, tired of his one-track mind.

The blond man moved off. Her attention shifted to Walker, whose gaze locked on her and went dark before he looked away.

He stopped jumping rope and lifted an arm to swipe across his forehead. Jen couldn't tear her gaze away from the strip of rigid tanned abdomen bared by his shirt. He traded places with Shep at the chin-up bar. Jen watched the ripple of muscles in Walker's arms as he reached up to grab the bar. Her mouth went dry and she felt as though steam were coming off her body.

Lust fogging her brain, she realized Shep had said something to her. She stopped punching. "Sorry, what?"

He grinned as though he knew exactly what she'd been thinking. "Heard you and McClain set a record at SWAT training the other day. I would've liked to have seen that."

"We did all right." Remembering again the searing heat in Walker's eyes when he'd come upon her behind the training center, Jen tried not to squirm.

"Think that was beginner's luck?"

"No," Walker said gruffly, before Jen could answer. "It's because we're good."

Surprised, Jen smiled at him and when he smiled in return, she melted a little.

It wasn't until he turned away that her brain engaged fully. *What* was wrong with her? She was here to do a job, she reminded herself. And she wasn't getting it done while in the same room with Mr. SWAT Stud.

He and the other two men would probably be in here for a while longer. She had planned to search both Farris's and Walker's lockers, and this might be her best chance to snoop.

After pulling off her handwraps and tucking them into the pocket of her shorts, she grabbed her towel and water bottle, and headed toward the door.

"You already done?" Shep asked.

"Yeah. I was in here long before you slackers," she joked.

The three men grunted. Walker nodded a goodbye, just as he'd done each day after their SWAT exercise.

Because they were both in the firehouse, he couldn't avoid her, but since that moment behind the training center, he had been…careful. He hadn't been around her more than was absolutely necessary. Was he skittish because of what had happened between them? Jen was, but she didn't have the option to avoid him.

She did a quick pass through the downstairs area. The

captain was in his office on the phone, and the other fire-fighters were out back, playing basketball.

She hurried upstairs and, with one last look around, slipped inside the men's locker room. The row of red lockers stood against the opposite wall. McClain's name was plainly marked on one close to the far end. The lockers had no locks and Jen opened his carefully in case the hinges squeaked the way hers did.

There wasn't a lot inside. A pair of tennis shoes, a shaving kit full of toiletries, a couple of T-shirts and a New York Yankees baseball cap. Beneath that, she saw the corner of a photograph. Listening to be sure no one was coming up the metal stairs, she slid the picture from under the cap and discovered what she thought was one photo was actually two.

The first showed Walker wearing a tux. *My, my, my,* she thought. He looked dark and suavely sexy, like an after-five cologne ad. The cut of the stark black fabric emphasized his broad shoulders and long legs. The whiteness of his shirt turned his skin a golden bronze and brought out the deep green in his eyes. But what really made Jen weak in the knees were his dimples. She would have loved to see him smile like that. If he ever intentionally set out to get her attention, she'd be a goner.

He stood next to a pretty blond woman with dark eyes, the two of them talking to a bride and groom. The bride had beautiful curly red hair, and the groom bore a striking resemblance to Walker. Handsome, tall, the same smoothly planed jaw. The fire-investigator brother he'd talked about, Jen surmised. So, who was the blonde?

The second photograph made clear she wasn't the sister Walker had mentioned the other day. In the shot, he held her from behind, his hands resting on her very pregnant belly.

A gold chain glinted at her neck, and her head was turned so that they were looking at each other. Though they were laughing, there was a tenderness in Walker's expression that put a sharp knot in Jen's chest. This was his wife. He had clearly adored the woman.

The expression on his face made him look like a completely different man. He was still gorgeous, but there was none of the hardness Jen had come to realize was in his green eyes more often than not. None of the grimness, the aloneness she hadn't realized until now had become a part of his features. It was the same man, on the outside anyway. But inside? Jen didn't know that man.

Staring at the picture, Jen felt as though she was invading his grief. His pain. She didn't belong there; no one did.

She knew she was supposed to learn everything about him she could, get inside his head if possible, but this seemed wrong.

Some things were private and should be kept that way. She wanted to stop, wrestled with the urge for a long moment, but she couldn't. She made herself replace the photos and search the small top shelf of the locker. There was a set of keys, two cans of shaving cream and a pair of white shoelaces. A heaviness settled over her.

She quietly closed the locker and slipped out of the room, going across the hall to the women's bunk room. Once inside, she sank down on the edge of her neatly made bed.

Tears prickled the backs of her eyes. Realizing the depth of Walker's loss—his entire world, his entire *future*—she found it hard to breathe for a moment.

That kind of suffering made a damn good case for turning vigilante. Had he? Jen had no idea if Walker was the Payback Killer, but after seeing those pictures, she wouldn't blame him if he was.

* * *

For the rest of her shift, Jen couldn't get the image of Walker and his wife out of her head, the glimpse she'd had of the man he used to be. She'd been so rattled by Walker's pictures, she had left the men's locker room before searching Farris's locker. She'd had to return a few minutes later to check his storage compartment and found nothing incriminating there.

Just because he was on the same shift schedule as Walker, she couldn't assume he'd been off the same days. Farris could've filled in for another firefighter. But a check of the work schedule on the dates of the murders showed he hadn't.

Even after heading home at shift's end, she spent way too much time thinking about the picture of Walker and a pregnant Holly. The haunted look he now wore in his eyes had Jen wanting to ask him about his wife.

The tightness in her chest was still there that afternoon as she accompanied Shelby Jessup to the fire investigator's office for a newspaper interview. The reporter was doing an article on women in the fire department, and he wanted to speak with Shelby, as well as Terra Spencer, Presley's first and only female fire investigator. She was also Jack Spencer's wife.

Shelby had invited Jen along so she could meet Terra. Jen liked Shelby, but she didn't want to get too close to the woman or anyone else. Still, she needed to take advantage of every possible opportunity she had to learn more about her primary suspect, so she had accepted.

Shelby pulled her car up to a redbrick building, telling Jen it had been Presley's original fire station. A weathered metal sign marked Fire Investigator hung over the glass door, and the title was repeated in black lettering on the door itself.

Though the building's electrical wiring and plumbing

had been updated several years ago, the exterior remained the same, lending an antique charm to the place.

Jen followed Shelby inside, immediately catching the faint odor of smoke and chemicals. She looked past a worn secretary's desk to a small office, separated from the front area by glass walls.

Down the hall was a dry-erase board on wheels, covered with photographs of fire scenes. A doorway across from the board was marked Fire Investigator.

"Presley has two fire investigators," Shelby told Jen. "Terra Spencer and Collier McClain."

"McClain?"

"Yeah. He's Walker's brother."

Jen nodded, smiling as a tall, striking woman with red-gold hair strode out of her office to greet them. "Hi, Shelby." "Hi."

After Shelby introduced Jen, Terra smiled at her. "I understand you're also a SWAT medic."

"Yes."

"Very impressive. Even more so because you're pretty."

Jen understood what Terra meant. There were still men in the fire department who resented women firefighters. If the woman was attractive, it was even more difficult to prove herself and be accepted.

Terra and Shelby were both pretty. Jen wouldn't have been surprised to learn that either or both had experienced trouble being accepted in a profession that was traditionally all male.

Terra returned to her office and dragged out one of two wooden armchairs. "Darla, my secretary, is taking a late lunch, so we can talk out here. My office is too small, plus there are files I don't want the reporter around."

She situated the chair to face the front desk, while Shelby retrieved the other one from Terra's office and did the same.

The door opened and a man who looked about Jen's age stepped inside, followed by an older, heavyset man who was carrying a camera.

Dressed in neatly pressed khakis and a white dress shirt, the first man smiled at Terra. "Investigator Spencer, I'm Don Frost. This is Randy Cook, my photographer. Thanks for taking the time to see me."

"You're welcome." She touched Shelby's shoulder. "Here's your other subject and this—" she gestured toward Jen "—is Jen Lawson, the newest firefighter in our department. She's also a SWAT medic."

"Nice to meet you both." He shook hands with Shelby and Jen.

Terra indicated the chairs she'd brought from her office. "We can talk here. How would you like to begin?"

"I'd like to get some background first." The man's gaze swung to Jen. "I'd like to talk to you also, if you're willing."

Since it didn't endanger her investigation, she nodded. "All right."

After several minutes of speaking with Terra, the reporter glanced at Jen. "Perhaps you could tell me exactly what a SWAT medic does."

She nodded and stood behind the chair next to his, then gave him a basic outline of a tactical medic's function. He asked her several questions before turning to Terra.

"Were you the one who implemented the SWAT medic program?"

"Myself and Collier McClain, the other fire investigator. It was a joint effort with Presley's police department. So far, the program has worked very well."

The front door creaked open and a tall, handsome man walked in. With his dark hair and rangy build, Jen thought he looked like Walker.

Terra smiled at him. "Here he is now. Collier McClain, meet Don Frost, a reporter with the *Presley Gazette*."

The man rose and stepped over to shake McClain's hand. "Would you have a few minutes to talk to me after I finish with the ladies? I'd like to get your take on working with women firefighters."

"Sure." McClain had a nice baritone voice, but it didn't make Jen's stomach flutter the way his brother's did.

"Great." Frost sat and turned his attention back to Jen and Terra.

Behind her, Jen heard Shelby greet Collier. After a few more minutes, the reporter finished with Jen and she re-joined Shelby, who was standing next to Collier.

Shelby tipped her head toward Jen. "Collier, this is Jen Lawson."

"Ah, you're my brother's new partner." Dusky green eyes twinkling, he extended his hand. "Sorry about that."

"I'm managing." She returned his smile, surprised to see dimples in the same place as Walker's, although Collier looked as if his smile came much easier than his brother's. The man was every bit as hunky as Walker.

Collier slid one hand into the front pocket of his navy uniform pants. "He's told me about you."

Jen arched a brow. "Should I be worried?"

"No. At least not yet." He grinned. "It's nice to finally meet you. Seems you've made an impression on him."

"I'm afraid to ask if it was good or bad," she joked, hoping her leading statement would prompt him to tell her more.

Just as he started to say something, his cell phone rang. He dug it out of his other pants pocket and looked at the display. His eyes twinkled. "Speak of the devil. Be right back."

He flipped open his phone and moved a few feet away. "What's going on?"

Dang it. What impression had she made on Walker? Good? Bad? She wanted to know what he had said about her to his brother.

Shelby sat in the empty chair and began her interview with Frost. Jen stayed where she was, trying to appear as if she were paying attention to the interview, but really listening to Collier's side of the conversation with his brother.

"—I went by your house before lunch and you weren't there," Collier said. "Where were you?"

After a pause, he asked, "Why?"

Where had Walker gone after their shift ended this morning? Jen wondered. To track down his next victim?

Collier listened for a moment, then said, "Did you get any sleep? Go on over to the house. Kiley and I always have a bed for you. If she isn't there, let yourself in."

The possibility that Walker might have been in Payback Killer mode made Jen uncomfortable, but that was what she was undercover to figure out.

"Well, next time, call me or Shea or somebody," Collier demanded, as he moved over to the far wall.

From Walker, Jen knew Shea was their sister. Thanks to Collier's distance and the reporter directing Shelby and Terra as his photographer took pictures, Jen couldn't hear anything else. She glanced over her shoulder as McClain flipped his phone shut.

Don Frost turned his attention to Jen. "Ms. Lawson, would you mind if my photographer got a shot of you?"

Her picture couldn't show up in the paper. She smoothed a hand down her ponytail as though concerned about her appearance. "I'd rather not."

"All right, no picture, but are you still okay with me using your interview in the article?"

"Yes."

The reporter then turned to Collier and asked if they could talk now.

As Walker's brother led the way down the short hallway to his office, Jen heard him say, "Investigator Spencer is one of the best investigators I've ever seen, male or female."

Terra laughed. "He's only saying that because I taught him everything he knows."

That got a chuckle from everyone as the men stepped inside McClain's office.

After a few more minutes of small talk with Terra, Jen and Shelby left. As they drove toward Jen's apartment, Jen turned to the other woman. "Have you been friends with the McClains a long time?"

"Several years, though longer with Collier. We used to be at the same station house, and a few years ago he worked a fire murder investigation with my husband, Clay, who's a detective."

"Is that the case where you were nearly killed?"

The other woman looked surprised. "How did you hear about that?"

"Farris. I didn't believe him at first, so I asked Walker about it and he confirmed."

"The guy's in prison now, thanks to Clay and Collier. As for Walker, he and I didn't become really good friends until after his brother's wedding. That was where my husband and I got together, and where Walker and his wife, Holly, did, as well."

"Did he and Holly know each other before?"

"No. She was a friend of the bride, Kiley."

Jen wondered if further questions would make Shelby wonder about the extent of Jen's interest in Walker, but she needed to know as much about him as possible. "How long did they date?"

"Less than two months, then they got married. They both said they knew the minute they met that they wanted to spend their lives together."

"That sounds romantic, but impulsive. Walker doesn't strike me as the type."

"He isn't. Or wasn't." Shelby smiled. "He used to be a dating machine and was never serious about anyone. Evidently Holly was the same, but once they met, that was it for both of them. They had been single long enough to recognize things were different that time. They were crazy about each other and dead certain about getting married."

It had taken Jen and Mark longer than two months to get to that point, but they'd been certain, too.

"About two months later, Holly found out she was pregnant and then…" Shelby's voice trailed off. "Have you heard about what happened to her? That she was murdered, probably for the necklace she was wearing?"

"Yes." Jen's throat went tight again as the photograph of Walker and his wife flashed through her brain.

"He's been trying to find her murderer ever since. Collier thinks he's obsessed."

"Do you?" Jen watched her friend carefully.

"I don't know. If I were in his shoes, I think I'd be determined to find the killer, too. He spends a lot of time trying to track down leads."

"He interviews people or reads police reports or what?"

"All of that, plus he visits homeless camps all around this area."

"That sounds like it could be dangerous."

Shelby nodded. "I think so, too. He also regularly contacts pawnshops, looking for that necklace."

Was it the chain Jen had seen Holly wearing in the photo?

They fell silent for a moment then Shelby slid a look at Jen. "He's a great-looking guy."

Jen met the other woman's gaze. "No argument here."

"He's also a great guy." Shelby braked at a stoplight. "Since Holly's murder, he hasn't been even close to the same man he was before. It's not that he's grim or hard, but something inside him switched off. I'm not sure how to explain it. I just know he isn't the same."

Thinking back to the photo Jen had seen—the easy smile, the openness in his face—she completely agreed. "Does he ever talk about the murder?"

"Maybe to Shep or his brother. Not to me. It would be wonderful if he could move on with someone new."

"Yes," Jen murmured, squashing a ridiculous fleeting urge that it could be her.

"Maybe someone he works with," Shelby said nonchalantly, as the car began moving again.

Jen shook her head.

"Don't try to deny it," the other woman said with a grin. "You're interested in him."

She was, but she shouldn't be. Not romantically anyway. "Well…"

"Word about your SWAT training session has gotten around. The guys say you two are good together."

"Working together is different than playing together."

Jen already felt a connection to her partner that, despite her physical jitteriness around him, seemed as though it had been years in the making, rather than days.

Shelby changed lanes. "Are you involved with someone back in Tulsa?"

"No, not now."

"It went bad?"

Jen never gave out details. People either didn't understand mental illness or felt she should've handled the situation with Mark differently. "You could say that."

After a long moment, the other woman said quietly, "Maybe you and Walker have more in common than just being SWAT medics."

"Maybe," Jen murmured.

Though the circumstances hadn't been similar, they had both lost someone they loved. Walker's loss had been unexpected and shockingly brutal. Jen's had been day by day, like a death drawn out for months. In the end, she hadn't been able to tough it out. Walker had. He still *was*. Even though she'd known him less than two weeks, Jen knew he wouldn't stop until he found Holly's murderer. And doing that kept him living in the past. At least Jen had been able to move forward, although she'd felt emotionally paralyzed for almost two years.

She didn't sense a ruthless need for revenge lurking inside Walker, but she'd missed seeing things right in front of her before.

It had taken her months to realize the severity of Mark's illness. In the beginning, the symptoms had come too infrequently for her to see a pattern, but not toward the end.

She brought her thoughts back to Walker. Jen was gathering information on him, like she was supposed to, but her interest in him went beyond that.

Regardless of her investigation, she wanted to know about Walker McClain. *Everything* about him.

Searching for his wife's necklace and regularly checking the homeless population confirmed he was a man who was still focused on his wife's murder. A man who wanted to have something his wife cherished that was taken from her.

As a woman, Jen found his devotion touching. And wildly

attractive. As an investigator, she had to look at his mind-set as obsessive and recognize it could also be that of a vigilante. Behavior that could easily be considered incriminating.

She didn't want to believe Walker was the Payback Killer, but the investigator in her had to run this show. She couldn't get sucked in by her emotions.

Chapter 5

The woman made him twitchy. Walker hadn't been able to get Jen out of his head since seeing her in the workout room.

He knew what his problem was, he admitted as he drove to the firehouse for the second day-on of their shift. His new partner had kick-started his libido after that SWAT exercise, and seeing her in the station's workout room two days ago had revved it into overdrive.

He had tried everything to push the image of her luscious curves out of his mind—running, fishing, mowing his lawn. He hadn't slept with a woman in two and a half years. He needed sex, just not with *her*. It needed to be with someone who didn't cause this hot tightness in his chest. So, last night he'd gone to a couple of the bars he'd frequented before meeting Holly.

Ultimately, he'd left alone. He hadn't been able to make himself go home with either of the women who'd offered, and he sure as hell wasn't taking any woman to his and Holly's house. It was just as well that he'd been solo, considering he had failed to work up enough interest to do more than chat.

He didn't have that problem with Jen. He had interest rushing through every vein in his body. Thoughts of her were taking up so much room in his head that he even imagined he'd smelled her tantalizing floral scent in the men's locker room after that workout. He needed to stay away from her whenever possible, he decided as he parked his SUV behind the firehouse and climbed out.

Brett Farris pulled into the space beside his at the same time a cab stopped at the curb. Jen got out and paid the driver, then started toward the station house.

Before Walker could ask her what was going on, Farris jumped in. "Car trouble?"

"Yes." A look of disgust crossed her features as she drew even with the two of them.

Farris fell into step beside her. "After our shift ends tomorrow, I'll take you home and look at it for you."

After a quiet "hey" to Walker, Jen said to the other man, "I think I'll just call a mechanic and see if he'll pick it up."

"I don't mind," Farris insisted. "On the way to your place, we can stop for breakfast."

"No, thanks," she said tightly.

"The offer stands if you change your mind."

She didn't respond.

Walker read loud and clear that she wouldn't. He should offer to help her with her vehicle. She was *his* partner, after all. But she appeared to have things under control.

As they left training classes that afternoon, he overheard Farris badgering her again. The firefighter kept offering to take her home or fix her car. Jen never lost her temper, but Walker could tell it was wearing on her. It was dang sure wearing on him. And his decision to keep some distance between them began to seem less important.

Well after dark, the burly firefighter was rechecking the curb jumpers, extra sections of hose that typically lay on the curb during use and were stored in one of the compartments on the captain's side of the truck. Jen was sweeping the bay.

Walker heard Farris start in on her for the fourth time, and some piece of his control popped loose. Jen was perfectly capable of handling the other man on her own, but Walker didn't care.

He stepped around the back of the engine where he had been inspecting the wide hose stored on top. Before he could tell his coworker to back off, Jen walked up to the other man.

"Knock it off, okay? Really."

Walker couldn't see her face, but the sternness in her voice had Farris stiffening. "I'm just trying to help."

"She's covered," Walker said. "We've worked it out."

Shooting him an irritated look, the other man finished bundling a small hose, stored in the same compartment as the curb jumpers. Binding the hose pack made it easier to carry up a ladder if other lines couldn't reach inside a burning structure. Farris's avid gaze slid down Jen's body one last time.

As the big man turned away, she looked at Walker and mouthed "Thanks." She looked so relieved, he wondered why he hadn't said something earlier.

He knew why the next morning when their shift ended and she slid into the passenger seat of his silver SUV. The velvety softness of her skin had him wanting to touch, and

Walker knew he should've stuck to his plan about staying away from her when possible.

As they started toward her apartment north of town, she smoothed a hand over the black leather seat and the wood dash panel. "Very nice."

"Thanks." He didn't see how she could smell so good after twenty-four hours on duty, but she did.

She rested her head back against the seat. His gaze trailed down the elegant line of her neck, lingered on her breasts for a second.

She turned her head toward him. "I appreciate your help with Farris. He just wouldn't stop."

The way she smiled had Walker's body going tight. Annoyed by his reaction, he shrugged. "That's what partners do."

He realized how abrupt he sounded when her eyes shuttered against him, but she didn't appear too upset when she said smartly, "Well, I'll be happy to rescue you from Farris anytime you need it."

Her breezy words got a chuckle out of him.

She half-turned in her seat to face him, pushing a loose strand of hair back into her braid. Walker was hit all over again by the pure liquid blue of her eyes. And he noticed the faint shadows of fatigue there.

"Did you do much yesterday?" she asked. "I went with Shelby to a newspaper interview at the fire investigator's office."

"Oh, yeah, my brother said he saw you there."

"I enjoyed meeting him."

"He said the same about you."

That wasn't all Collier had said. Walker had spent hours trying to get Jen out of his head, then his brother had started in about liking her and suggesting Walker ask her out. He *wasn't* asking her out. He wasn't spending any non-work-related time with her. Well, except for now.

"What did you do on our day off?" she asked again.

"Mowed my lawn. I went fishing, too. The ones I caught were too small to keep so I threw them back." The one thing he couldn't seem to throw was thoughts of her.

"Were you gone all day?"

"Pretty much."

"Did you hear about that meth dealer the police found this morning, just before our shift ended?"

Walker nodded as they left behind the older, more populated area of town and neared the north edge of Presley's city limits. There were several new housing additions up this way now, as well as a new apartment complex.

"They reported on the radio that the cops believe it's another murder by the Payback Killer," she said.

"Yeah. Just like the others, he was killed first then burned, using the flashbang to start the fire."

"I wonder if the killer meant to blow up that guy's mobile meth lab. The grenade could've accidentally gone off if he had been close enough to the victim's car."

"I bet it wasn't an accident. The Payback Killer probably didn't care about the explosion. This way, he killed two birds with one stone." The back of his hand accidentally brushed Jen's resting on top of the console.

He sounded so sure that her nerves prickled. Was he only supposing the killer hadn't cared about causing an explosion? Or did he know that for a fact because *he* was the one who'd detonated the grenade so close to the volatile chemicals?

The meth dealer's time of death hadn't been determined yet. The only thing within almost a mile of that area was a homeless camp, and no one there wanted the cops circling around. The blaze had been out well before the fire department was ever called to clean up the toxic murder scene. How long had the newest victim been dead before then? Could it have been as many as twenty-four hours before the fire murder was reported?

Jen had learned from eavesdropping on his brother's phone conversation that Walker had been MIA for some of those hours. Would his absence coincide with the victim's time of death when it was released?

It was a possibility Jen couldn't dismiss. Where had he been during that time? Trolling the streets for another lowlife to kill?

Jen didn't like either scenario. "These last two murders happened pretty close together," she observed.

"Maybe the dead guys were released from prison within a day or two of each other. So far what we know about this victim's murder follows the pattern of the others. He'd been convicted of making meth and was probably back to doing it right after his release."

"In which case, he deserved it?"

His shrug didn't tell her anything except that he thought the victim was scum, just like he'd thought about the others before him. She believed that, too.

"Is the Payback Killer murdering all these men the same way?" she asked.

"I don't know about the meth dealer, but the other four were strangled then set on fire using a flashbang."

She touched his arm. "It's the next right turn."

At the feel of her hand, Walker felt sensation zip through him. He tensed. All she'd done was touch his arm. Big deal.

Irritated, he turned into the lot of a new apartment complex and drove around the front building to one on the side. Her Wrangler sat in front of building B. More aware of her than he liked as they climbed out of his car, he wasted no time popping open the hood of her vehicle.

"I'm going to check your battery and cables first," he said.

"Okay." She stood quietly several feet away.

The cables were clean and tight. He straightened and peered at her around the hood. "They look good. Now I need you to tell me if there's gas in your tank."

Her eyes narrowed. "Are you kidding me?"

He couldn't help a grin. "Hey, you'd be surprised how many people don't pay attention to their gas gauge. Sometimes a no-start problem is as easy as putting in fuel."

"Well, I do pay attention and yes, there's gas in my truck."

"Okay. Flip on your headlights, then when I tell you, turn the ignition key." He stepped back for a better view.

She opened the automobile's door and reached in to follow his instructions.

The headlights flared on.

"Okay, now turn the key."

She did, and the lights went out. She craned her neck around the door to see him. "Did that tell you anything?"

"Yeah. It's a bad battery."

She grimaced. "Is there a mechanic around here you recommend?"

"You don't need one. This is a simple problem, one I can fix." Where the hell had *that* come from?

She looked as surprised as he felt. "That's really nice, but—"

"It's no big deal." Why couldn't he shut up? It was as though someone else was talking. "If I do it, it'll save you having to wait on towing it to a garage for repair and probably a diagnostic charge, as well."

"Thanks. That would be great."

Her smile reached right into his gut and twisted. "I won't be able to replace it until this evening."

"That's fine. Wonderful. I just appreciate you offering."

Why had he done that? Walker asked himself. Seeing the relief on her face, Walker knew it didn't matter why. He had offered. He would do it. Besides, the sooner Jen's vehicle was fixed, the sooner she could get to and from work on her own.

That suddenly seemed really important when she moved up beside him, her flirty scent teasing him.

He found himself wanting to get even closer, bury his face in her neck and just breathe her in.

Walker could deny wanting her, but what was the point? His attraction to her wasn't fading as he'd hoped it would. Instead, it was starting to feel much, much bigger than him.

He wrestled all day with whether or not to return to Jen's. He was the one who'd offered to fix her car, but did it really have to be *him?*

He'd thought about paying a mechanic to pick up her Wrangler, but he couldn't bring himself to back out. It pissed him off that he couldn't seem to get a grip on his lust, and he was determined to prove to himself that he could spend time with her by ignoring the charge she set off inside him.

So, a little after six o'clock that evening, he knocked on the door to her upstairs apartment. Her building consisted of eight units, four upstairs and four down, with the breezeway between bisected by a metal staircase. Her apartment was on the front half of the building.

He would change out her battery then leave. There would be no thoughts of her naked or nearly naked. No wondering how soft her lips were. Or what she tasted like. Just battery in, leave.

That resolve took a hit when she opened her door. She wore snug jeans and a fitted pink T-shirt that bared a narrow strip of her tanned flat stomach. Her hair was down, the thick wavy mass flowing around her shoulders like black silk. He hadn't seen her hair down before. The way it framed her face made her features appear china-doll delicate. He wanted to put his hands in her hair, feel it slide through his fingers.

It took all his focus to make himself remember he was supposed to care only about her car.

"Hi." Her cheeks were flushed, her eyes sparkling. "I really appreciate this."

"No problem." His voice sounded rusty. "I'd better get started."

"Okay." She locked and shut her door, following him back through the breezeway and out to the parking lot. "Have you eaten yet? I could order a pizza."

"I'm okay. Thanks, though."

Why was she coming with him? There was no good reason for it. Nor was there a reason for her *not* to come.

It was no big deal. They were partners, period. And they were good together. Walker wasn't going to mess that up. And he wasn't going to let Jen mess *him* up. He could do this.

"Is there anything I can help with or should I stay out of the way?"

You can stay way over there. Walker bit back the words. He was not going to get all hot and bothered. "You can hang around if you want. It's pretty boring work."

"I won't feel right if I leave you out here alone. Could I get you something to drink?"

"Not yet." Pulling on a pair of latex gloves he'd taken from his blow-out pack to protect his hands from battery acid, he popped the hood and began loosening the negative cable. "Maybe in a bit."

"You don't mind if I watch?"

Hell, yes, he did, but he wasn't letting on. "It's okay."

She was quiet, and after he explained how he would remove the battery, she stayed at the corner of the truck. There was a good two feet between them, but Walker could feel the heat of her body. He shifted his shoulders against a sudden restlessness.

In an effort to keep his mind from going to places it shouldn't, he tried to think of something to talk about. He'd never had this much trouble talking to a woman. Or doing anything else with them. He knew Jen had no siblings and he remembered she'd told the woman they'd rescued from the bathtub that she had no grandparents.

Using the clamp puller, he removed the negative cable. "How long did you live in Tulsa?"

"My whole life."

"Do you have family there?"

"An aunt." Her prolonged pause had him looking up from loosening the positive terminal clamp. "We aren't very close."

Her words were careful, her tone neutral, but he sensed pain there.

"Did you leave anyone else behind?"

"Like a boyfriend?"

Yes. Walker shrugged.

"No."

"You didn't date much over there?" He couldn't believe he was trying to pull information out of her.

Tracing a finger along the edge of the Jeep's hood, she studied him thoughtfully, as if trying to decide something. "I was engaged once."

Whoa. Walker straightened so fast, he nearly hit his head on the upraised hood. "Really?"

"You find that surprising?" Her voice was light, teasing, but he felt a sudden tension in her.

"No, of course not." As he removed the positive clamp, something heavy settled in his chest. He had an insane urge to touch her hand. "Things didn't work out?"

"No."

The raw unguarded pain in her eyes surprised him. And had him biting off further questions. Had her fiancé died? Broken their engagement? Had *she* broken it?

Whatever had happened, she was still carrying it around. He sure as hell understood that. The brief haunted look in her eyes matched what he'd experienced when he lost Holly, and he felt something completely nonphysical connect between him and Jen.

He wanted to know more, a lot more, but she obviously didn't want to talk about it. This burning curiosity about her was exactly why he hadn't been able to go home with either of those women at the bar last night. Still, he didn't ask the questions he wanted to ask.

After removing the hold-down hardware, he lifted the battery out of its tray and set it on the ground beside him. He installed the new one and began to reattach the hardware.

She leaned in closer, sweeping her hair to the other shoulder. Walker's gaze followed, skimming over her porcelain skin, the pale blue veins running beneath. If he wanted, he could reach out and slide his finger down the length of her creamy neck.

"On the next shift, I'm supposed to cook."

"Yeah?" Her change of topic told him he'd been right not to try and get more information. Despite the low thrum of awareness in his blood, he grinned. "Are you thinking about bribing me to do it?"

"Not after you've been so great to help with my car. Actually, I was wondering if you could help me with the groceries." She wrinkled her nose. "I don't know what to buy. Or how much."

"Are you trying to make a good impression?" He installed the positive battery cable, then the negative one. "If you do, you'll never get out of cooking again."

"Good point, but I think I should at least try not to humiliate myself."

"Make something easy that feeds a lot of people."

"*Make* something? Get out of here! I was thinking frozen pizza and Twinkies."

He laughed. "You serve that and you *will* need help. I don't want to have to break in another partner."

"Gee, thanks," she muttered.

"I'll help you." He sprayed the terminals with a corrosion preventative, keenly aware of the stroke of her long fingers along the Jeep's hood, the sweet curve of her denim-hugged hip, the golden-red glow of the sunset streaking her hair.

It took a moment for him to realize he was finished. He had to make himself move, picking up the old battery and carrying it to his SUV. After placing it on some newspaper he'd unfolded on the floor in the back end, he peeled off his latex gloves and tossed them alongside the battery before returning to where she stood.

She smiled. "That's it?"

"Yep." He drew in a deep breath of her soft feminine scent, growing hot under the collar of his T-shirt. "Your truck should start now."

"So, I don't have to wait for anything to dry or set or season?"

He laughed. "No. Just crank her up and let's see if she'll go."

"Oh." She gave him a sheepish smile.

She was so pretty. He was close enough that he could lean in and brush his mouth over hers.

"What?" She arched a brow. "You can't believe how clueless I am about cars?"

"It's not that." Until right then, he hadn't been aware he was staring. An ache bloomed in his chest. He didn't understand it, but he knew he should get away from her. Now.

Want hammered hard at him. Did she feel this pull, this electricity between them at all? Or was it only him?

"Go ahead," he said hoarsely. "Try to start it."

She leaned in, her position affording him a prime view of her backside cupped in those tight jeans. She turned the key and the engine hummed to life, sounding as good as new.

"Oh, wow!" She killed the engine and shut the door. "Thank you so much."

Her blue eyes shone at him and his nerves snapped taut. He couldn't stop his gaze from dropping to her mouth. He stared so long that she licked her lips nervously. His body tightened. A distant voice in his head demanded he leave.

"Walker?"

One step brought him within inches of her. He told himself to step back because if he didn't, he was going to—

"Oh, hell," he muttered, and kissed her.

She gave a tiny gasp and for a split second, he tried to hit his mental brakes. Then she melted into him. He wasn't stopping, wasn't sure he could.

He backed her up against the front quarter panel and took her mouth. She opened to him, her taste sweet and tangy. Wild.

He spread his legs, caging her in, although she didn't act as if she wanted to go anywhere. Her mouth was hot and slick, and Walker couldn't get enough of it. His pulse beat hard in every cell of his body. And when her tongue stroked his, it was as though she lit a fuse.

He went deeper, harder, into her mouth. He wanted inside her, on her.

He didn't know how long they kissed. When his chest began to ache, he finally lifted his head. One hand was in her hair, cupping the back of her skull and the other spread low on her back, pressing her hips to his.

His blood thundered in his ears. Only then did he realize her hands were clamped at his waist, holding tight. Her touch was hot through his T-shirt. The brilliant blue of her eyes, the pulse beating furiously in the hollow of her throat, had him wanting to start all over.

She was breathing hard, her lush breasts rising and falling against his chest. He wanted to put his hands on her there. Everywhere.

She looked as stunned as he felt. Lust throbbed hard in his veins. His hand involuntarily clenched in the thick satin of her hair. He wanted to bury his face in it, feel it slide over his skin.

What had he just done? It took two attempts before he could release her. He turned and sagged against the Jeep.

So did she. "Crap," she breathed.

That drew a startled laugh from him. "No one's ever said that after kissing me."

"I bet not," she murmured.

He turned his head. Her eyes were closed and his body jolted when she touched her tongue to her bottom lip as though she could still taste him there.

Every muscle in his body clenched, and he cursed under his breath. "Stop looking like that or I'll have to do it again."

"And we shouldn't do it again, right?" At the question in

her voice, she opened her eyes and looked straight at him. "I mean, we *shouldn't* do that again."

The resolve in her voice was lost beneath the sound of wonder. A sound that made Walker even hotter.

"Right. We shouldn't. We won't." One taste of her wasn't going to be enough, but that was all he was getting. He straightened and stepped away from the vehicle, his legs feeling like sand. "I'd better go."

He'd been kidding himself to think he could bluff his way past this…lust, need, whatever it was. The guilt he felt because of his attraction to her was there in full force, but it hadn't done a damn thing to check the hunger that had shredded his common sense, his determination. He felt edgy, reckless. He had to put some distance between them.

Slamming the vehicle's hood shut, he started for his SUV, then realized he'd left his toolbox. He turned and bent to retrieve it, sharply aware that she was bracing herself against the Jeep with one hand, as though she needed help to stand. Her eyes followed him hotly.

As he hefted the box and moved past her toward his car, she said, "Thanks again. I really appreciate it. I owe you."

In the old days, he would've thrown out some flirty remark or a funny one, but his mind was a big blank slate. He was out of practice. "No," he said quickly. "You don't. You don't owe me anything."

Deep down, he liked the idea of her being in his debt. He knew exactly what he wanted, and he also knew he wasn't going to take it.

Walker said goodbye and drove away. His body burning, he slammed a fist against the steering wheel. He'd gone there to prove he could spend time with her without giving in to the hard-edged want between them.

So what if he hadn't done everything he wanted to

her? He'd kissed her, which was way more than he
should've done.

He had to face the facts. He didn't have control over a
damn thing regarding Jen Lawson.

Chapter 6

Amazing. As Walker drove away, Jen stayed plastered against the side of her Jeep. As much because her legs wouldn't work as because her brain had stalled out. But it shifted gears now, racing past the slow-as-honey flow of her blood. Oh, yes, her brain was working overtime now.

She should've moved. After that first startling brush of his mouth against hers, she should've stepped away. Or told him to stop.

Instead, she'd kissed him back. It was dangerous. Borderline stupid. And she wasn't nearly as sorry as she should have been.

Her body was tuned up tighter than a steel-stringed guitar. Mark had been the best kisser she'd ever known, until now. Walker McClain had blown every thought out of her head and literally buckled her knees.

She had grabbed on to his taut waist at first because she

was surprised, then she'd held on tight because her legs had turned to rubber. He hadn't said the kiss was a mistake, hadn't tried to apologize, and she was glad. She didn't want him to apologize.

They'd agreed not to do it again and she could pull that off. All she had to do was keep it from looping through her mind like a broken tape. Right.

If she wasn't investigating him, she would—

Stop. Just stop. She *was* investigating him, and the time she spent with him had to be used to find out if he was the Payback Killer. This job was tricky, no matter the identity of the suspect. With McClain, it was like walking blind into a minefield. But she could do it. She *had* to do it.

She repeated that to herself four days later as they walked into the grocery store. Back on duty after their days off, she had put out sandwich makings for lunch. Responding to two medical calls, a car accident with injury and an automatic alarm, had kept them busy until around five o'clock.

As promised, Walker was helping her shop for food. After their kiss, she had wondered if he might back out, if things would be weird between them. Except for an initial moment of awkwardness when they saw each other the next day at SWAT practice, things had been fine.

The kiss was there between them. She knew he was as aware of it as she was, but it wasn't in the way. Yet.

As he wheeled a shopping cart in front of them down the bread aisle, he glanced at her. "I saw Farris working out with you this morning, before we got our first call. Was he bothering you?"

"Not too much. He wanted to know if I'd had any trouble getting to work. I told him no, that you fixed my battery." She rolled her eyes. "He said he would 'fix my battery' any time I wanted."

Walker stopped, bringing Jen up short. "Did he make a move?"

"No, no. He's ninety-nine percent talk."

"Well, he's been 'talking' since your first day. If you have any trouble with him, you let me…let the captain know."

Warmed by his defense of her, she nodded, surprised to see a flash of the same heat that had been in his eyes before he'd kissed her. She added several loaves of French bread to the cart, then several of wheat and white.

As they continued on, her gaze wandered to his hands, so strong and dark on the cart's handle. She remembered how he'd cradled her scalp during their kiss, how his other hand had splayed low on her back, bringing her tight against him. The short sleeves of his uniform shirt revealed corded forearms dusted with black hair and biceps that she knew were steel-hard bands of muscle.

Want uncurled low in her belly. She was blisteringly aware of him. That was a factor of this assignment she'd accepted, but it was nothing she couldn't handle. To prove that to herself, she forced herself to look away from the strong column of his neck and the hint of chest hair in the open vee of his shirt.

She followed him as he turned down the row for pasta sauce. He recommended a brand and told her how many jars to get.

"I'm so glad you're not going to tell me to make the sauce, like you do."

As she placed the items in the cart, he asked, "You're coming to the shift party tomorrow, aren't you?"

"Yes. You'll have to tell me how to get to your house."

"All right." After a minute, he asked, "How long have you been a firefighter?"

"Ten years. How about you?"

"Eleven. I came on a couple of years after my brother. Ever want to do anything else?"

"For a while, I wanted to be a teacher."

"What made you change your mind?" As they made their way down another row, his gaze was fixed intently on her face, as though he really wanted to know.

And she wanted to tell him. Mostly. "My senior year in college, there was a fire in my sorority house. My boyfriend Mark and I were on the second floor and managed to get out along with everyone else except two girls. They were close to the exit but couldn't find it in the smoke. Mark went back in to help and the smoke overtook them. The firefighters had to go in after all of them."

"And?" His features were sober.

She heard the concern in his voice, the slight tension that said he knew, as did every firefighter, that things could've ended badly.

"Everyone was fine, but I had never felt so helpless. I was basically useless to Mark or anyone else. Those firefighters were amazing, and that's when I decided I wanted to be one. So, when Mark went to law school, I went to the fire academy."

"The two of you stayed together for a while?"

"Yes. We got engaged after I finished firefighting school." She added packages of lasagna noodles, placing them next to the bread.

"How long were you engaged?"

"Almost three years. We didn't want to get married until he finished law school."

"And did he finish?"

"Yes."

"From what you said the other night, it sounded like you two didn't get married."

"That's right." Telling him everything about Mark might get Walker to open up about his wife or how he'd coped after her murder, but Jen couldn't do it. "What about you? Did you ever think about being anything else?"

"No." His gaze burned into her, and she worried for a second he might ask more questions about Mark, but he didn't. "My story isn't nearly as interesting as yours."

Jen was plenty interested.

"I always wanted to be a firefighter. My brother and I are third-generation."

"You both followed in your father's footsteps. I think that's neat." It was another aspect of family she had never experienced.

As they walked, she scanned the list of ingredients he'd written down for her. She placed real Parmesan cheese and packages of mozzarella and ricotta cheese in the cart's seat, careful to keep the items separate from the sauce and bread. She continued down the refrigerated section toward the eggs and noticed Walker wasn't following.

She glanced over her shoulder to see him standing where she'd left him. "Did I forget something?"

He shook his head, gesturing at the basket. "Are you putting the food in some kind of order?"

"Yes," she answered before she thought better of it.

Amusement glinted in his eyes. "Really?"

"Really."

"What order?"

"Grains together, dairy with dairy, meat, eggs and—" She put a hand on her hip when he started laughing. "Why is that funny?"

"I've never known anyone who did that."

"Oh." His grin was so cute she couldn't help grinning in return. "Well, now you do."

"Yep. Why do you do it that way?"

"I just…do." Her aunt had insisted on "a place for everything and everything in its place." Jen knew her need for orderliness could be traced back to her upbringing. If she didn't hang up her clothes in the right order, or didn't put her toys back in the exact spot where she'd gotten them, she was disciplined.

She thought that might be why she agreed to work undercover. All her *T*s had to be crossed, all her *I*s dotted. She needed things to be right. She had worked hard to put her own life in order, but that had fallen apart when Mark became ill. Her world had become increasing disorder on a daily basis.

She tried to give Walker a mock glare, but couldn't manage it. "Stop laughing at me and tell me about your first call. If you can remember back that far."

"Very funny," he drawled. "That actually *is* an interesting story."

They stopped for eggs, and Jen made a place for them at the back of the cart with the other proteins. She ignored Walker's widening smile and the way his dimples deepened.

"It was a major rager, at night. Another guy and I were probies."

"Wow, your first call was a structure fire? That must've been incredible."

"It was. When we reached the scene, the captain told us to stay in the front of the truck and wait for instructions. I remember telling myself not to touch anything, and the next thing I know all heck breaks loose. Sirens and horns start going off and the two of us are looking around, trying to figure out the problem. Finally, we noticed that everyone is staring at our truck and the driver shouts, 'Probie, get off the damn footswitch!'"

Enjoying the way Walker's face lightened as he told the story, she chuckled.

"I'm not even to the good part yet." He grinned. "I started sweating because I figured I had just made a first-class fool out of myself, but when I looked down, it wasn't my foot on the horn and siren buttons. It was the other guy's. After that, the captain made us get out and direct traffic."

Jen was laughing outright now. "Are you sure it wasn't you with the big feet?"

"It wasn't, but it easily could've been. We were both green and stupid."

"That's a pretty good story." She moved ahead to the meat section.

After choosing two large packages of ground beef, she set them beside the eggs. A loaf of bread had somehow moved next to the eggs, so she rearranged it before picking up two more packages of meat. As she set them in the cart, she noticed the Parmesan cheese in the middle of the lasagna noodles. Her gaze shot to Walker's.

He looked questioningly at her then at the cart. "That's probably enough beef."

"Okay." Maybe things were sliding around on their own. She returned the cheese to its spot.

Next she placed two heads of lettuce in a corner of the cart. A package of lasagna noodles sat on top of the pasta sauce jars. She knew now these things weren't displacing themselves.

"Knock it off," she told him with a mock glare. "You're getting the food out of order."

"Out of order?" His dimples flashed, mischief clear in his green eyes. "I didn't know there was supposed to be an order."

She sniffed. "Shows what you know, Mr. Chef."

"Are we supposed to unpack them in a certain sequence? Cook them in order, too?"

"You're just hilarious."

"Me?" He laughed. "You're the one who's building the food pyramid in the grocery cart."

"Oh, be quiet." She chuckled as she walked a few steps to look at the tomatoes.

He bumped her hip lightly with the cart. "Tell me your first-call story."

"It's not nearly as funny as yours. We were dispatched to a fire in the woods. It was fall and there was a huge harvest moon. We even talked about it on the way to the scene. We got there and—"

A knowing grin stretched across his face.

"You guessed it. The moonlight was filtering through the man's trees, but the woods were so thick he couldn't see the whole moon. He only saw an orange glow."

"So he thought a fire was burning."

"Yes."

She smiled when he did. After picking up the remaining items she would need for meals until the end of their shift, she found a short checkout line.

Walker stopped the cart behind her and helped put the items onto the conveyor belt. Several minutes later, they had made the short drive to Station Three and were unloading the bagged groceries from the rescue truck.

Jen started inside with two full paper sacks then paused when she noticed Walker had stopped and was standing at the edge of the drive, staring hard at two men in front of Helping Hands shelter.

The rigid set of his body had her moving up beside him. "Everything okay?"

"Yeah, sure."

He sounded so distant, she glanced at him. His features were like granite, his eyes narrowed to glittering slits. What was he seeing? Jen wondered. She recognized one of the men as someone who worked there. The other was a stranger.

Walker's hands were clenched so tight his knuckles showed white. Why was he suddenly honed in on those men? Did it have anything to do with his wife's murder?

"Do you know those men?" she asked.

As though he suddenly remembered what he was doing, Walker abruptly turned and strode to the truck, gathering up the last two grocery bags and going into the firehouse.

With one last look at the men in front of the shelter, Jen followed, as concerned as she was curious.

Her partner's easygoing demeanor was gone, hidden behind a sharp-eyed, steely-jawed man who looked as grim as he had the first time she'd met him.

As they walked into the kitchen, she realized he hadn't answered her question. She asked another. "Are you sure you're okay?"

"I'm sure," he snapped.

Ouch. Jen managed not to wince, but her heart sank. She had thought they were finally making a real connection.

Real? she scoffed to herself. How real could it be when she was lying to him? Spying on him?

He began unloading groceries, and Jen could feel tension rolling off him. What was bothering him?

"Thanks for the help," she said. "I can take it from here."

His gaze shot to her as though he'd only just realized she was there.

His distance was like a slap in the face. And served to remind Jen exactly who she was. Who *he* was. What she was doing here.

No matter what their relationship appeared to be, she and Walker weren't friends. *Or anything else,* she added, when the memory of their kiss flashed through her mind.

She gave a small smile. "Why don't you go on? This won't take me a minute. You helped plenty by going with me to the store."

He continued to put away the food, practically seething with impatience. What had he been thinking while staring at the men in front of the shelter? He wasn't interested in sharing the answer with her. That couldn't have been more clear if "Keep Out" were tattooed on his forehead. Why wouldn't he talk to her? Because he didn't discuss certain things? Or because he had something to hide?

"If there's something else you want to do," she urged, "feel free. I might have to ask your help when I start the lasagna to help prevent any noodle disasters."

"I need to check on something. See you in a bit."

"All right."

Two seconds later, he was out of sight and Jen was silently cussing her head off.

Charmed by a layer of the man she thought she'd uncovered, she had forgotten the reality of the situation.

She was doing a job. A job that might eventually get him arrested for murder.

Detective Daly had called Jen this morning with a time of death for the meth dealer. Farris had an alibi which now eliminated him as a suspect, but Walker didn't. The space of time in question was the same space of time Jen had overheard Walker's brother ask him about. While he had been MIA, he would've had plenty of time to kill that meth dealer. Had he?

Jen didn't know. Right now, she felt as though she had no idea about anything concerning Walker McClain, but she told the detective that Walker's brother had been looking for him during the time in question.

She was disappointed at not learning anything new, but she was more disappointed because he had shut her out so completely. She had thought they were getting somewhere, but they weren't. And she had come dangerously close to forgetting the first rule of her job—no emotional involvement.

She had to remember she was investigating him, not dating him.

Walker knew something had changed between him and Jen, and it wasn't because of that kiss. It was because he'd been a jerk.

He finally admitted it the next evening. The shift party was in full swing in his backyard, and Walker's blue shift was slaughtering the green shift in volleyball. Jen tossed the ball high and set it for him. He spiked it hard across the net. Clay Jessup, Shelby's detective husband, had agreed to play for the other team and returned the volley. As the blue shift scored another point, Walker couldn't help grinding his teeth.

It seemed Shep touched Jen after every other point. A high five, a squeeze on the shoulder. Once he even lifted her to his shoulder for a victory lap. When in the hell had volleyball become so touchy-feely?

The frequent touches didn't appear to bother her. She looked as though she was having fun. Her face was flushed, her eyes a brilliant blue against the smooth golden tan of her face. Her skin glowed with a dewy sheen, from the elegant line of her neck to the plane of her chest, bared by a modestly cut sleeveless T-shirt. His gaze tracked over her prime backside and down the leanly muscled legs clad in slim sky-blue capris.

Walker jerked his gaze away. As hard as he was hitting the ball, he was surprised it wasn't flat, but Shep wasn't the main cause of his frustration. Walker was more annoyed at himself for the way he'd snapped at Jen the night before.

She didn't act mad, hadn't tried to avoid him or duck out of the party, but things between them were different.

He rotated out of the game and went to the deck to fire up both propane grills. Once they were hot, he began cooking hamburgers while Shelby's husband grilled chicken breasts. Groups of folding chairs sat under three of Walker's biggest oak trees to accommodate the firefighters and their guests. The picnic table, which seated six, was shaded under the covered part of the deck.

After a few minutes, Walker called everyone to eat. He and Clay piled cooked meat on a platter as people began to form a quasi-line.

Bowls of chips, potato salad and fruit sat at one end. Cups and a plastic dispenser of sweet tea sat at the other, and a cooler full of ice and drinks was situated beneath the table. Talking and laughing, people filled their plates, poured their drinks and sat down to eat.

Walker and Clay continued to grill meat until everyone had been served. Jen sat at the picnic table with Shep, Farris, Captain Yearwood and Shelby. Walker was keenly aware of Jen. Or rather how close Shep sat to her. From the corner of his eye, he saw his friend stand up and touch Jen on the shoulder then say something. She handed him her cup, and he also took the captain's.

He strode to the cooler, which sat a few feet away from where Walker stood.

As Shep refilled the cups with ice, he grinned over at Walker. "Come on and eat. There's still an empty place at the table."

"Yeah, I will in a second." He flipped over a half-done hamburger patty.

His gaze shifted to Jen as Shep returned to his seat, sliding in beside her before leaning in to say something.

As Walker watched them with their heads close together, his chest tightened. What were they talking about? Was Shep asking her out? He was a good guy. Jen might say yes. And Walker would hate it if she did. He had no right to feel that way—*he* sure as hell wasn't asking her out—but there it was.

Yesterday, he'd enjoyed spending time with her at the store, then he had ruined it when he zeroed in on the shelter's newest visitor. All he could think about was getting over there to talk to the man, see if he had the telltale scar across his knuckles. The man didn't, and he didn't know anyone who did. Frustration had burned through Walker. Would he ever get a break?

Afterward, he'd been too distracted at yet another letdown to register the subtle tension between him and Jen, but it had finally penetrated his thick skull.

Guilt had surfaced this morning for snapping at her. He told himself he didn't have to explain anything to her, but the urge kept scratching at him.

Clay shut off his grill and snagged a plastic cup full of tea. "All the chicken's cooked, so I'm going to eat with Shelby."

Walker nodded, pointing with his long spatula to the hamburgers still sizzling on his grill. "I'm almost finished here, too."

Taking a long drink, Clay's gaze shifted to the picnic table where Jen sat. "Shelby says you and your new partner are getting along great."

They had been, until last night when Walker had jumped down her throat. "Yeah."

"Just partners?"

Walker slid him a look. "What else?"

"She's a knockout."

"I'm sure your wife will be glad to know you think so."

The other man chuckled. "Don't you think she is?"

It was a long moment before he grudgingly said, "I have eyes." That was as close as he was getting to an admission.

"Have you thought about asking her out?"

Walker narrowed his eyes. "Have you been talking to my brother?"

Clay laughed. "No. Just wondering if you're interested."

"That wouldn't be a good idea."

"Ah, so you are. Shelby says you haven't been out with anyone since Holly died."

"Since when do people care so much about my social life?"

"I'm guessing since it started to look like you might get one."

Besides work and the occasional outing with his family, Walker hadn't had anything close to a social life in two and a half years. His shift party used to be an annual affair, but he hadn't had one since Holly's murder.

The man beside him grew serious. "But you're right. It's nobody's business."

If anybody knew grief, the conflicting emotions of guilt and anger, it was Clay. Not only had he lost his first wife to cancer, but his best friend, Shelby's brother, had been killed while they were mountain climbing.

Walker couldn't keep his gaze from going to Jen. "What Shelby said is true. I haven't been out with anyone."

He couldn't recall enjoying anything recently as much as he'd enjoyed grocery shopping with Jen. He'd gotten a kick out of watching her, talking to her, teasing her. The thought of her food-sorting method had him grinning inside.

"You'll know when it's time," Clay said.

Walker wasn't so sure. The only woman he was remotely interested in was Jen, and they had already agreed that anything between them wasn't a good idea because they worked together. But if they were to get involved, they wouldn't be breaking any rules. Fire department policy prohibited romantic relationships between firefighters and superior officers, not between firefighters.

That said, he liked having her as a partner and he didn't want to screw that up, which he might have already done by acting like an ass the night before.

He didn't feel as though he had to tell her everything, but if there were any bad feelings, they could get in the way of work. That could be dangerous, especially when they teamed up for SWAT calls. She deserved to know why he'd been so short with her.

He made the rounds to make sure everyone had enough to eat, and he was talking to a group of people under one of the trees when he saw Jen get up and go inside the house. A few seconds later, Farris followed her. Why?

Walker was halfway to the back door before he realized he'd moved, but he didn't stop.

He stepped into the kitchen, scanning the adjacent living room and the front entryway. There was no sign of Jen or Farris. A noise came from the hallway off the foyer where there were two guest bedrooms, a bathroom and a utility room. Stepping around the corner, he saw Jen open a bedroom door and peek inside.

"Everything okay?"

She gave a little jump, looking over her shoulder with an uncertain smile. "I'm looking for the bathroom."

He pointed past her. "Two doors down."

"Thanks."

He decided to wait for her in the kitchen. She'd have to come through there to get outside, and he could speak to her then.

When she appeared, he was leaning against the counter closest to the door.

She looked surprised to see him. "Hey."

"Hey. I wanted to talk to you for a minute."

"Okay." She looked as though she didn't have a clue why.

"About last night—"

The back door opened and Captain Yearwood boomed, "Is there any more ice?"

"Yeah, I'll get it." Walker grabbed another bag out of the freezer and passed it to the man.

Just as he closed the door, Farris strolled in from the foyer and walked through the kitchen. As he stepped out to rejoin the party, Shelby came inside and headed to the dining table where she had left a platter of cookies.

How many people were going to come in here? Walker thought in exasperation. He would have to wait to talk to Jen.

After removing the plastic wrap from the cookies, Shelby started back outside, telling Walker to bring his homemade ice cream. Jen swiped a cookie from the tray and grabbed a stack of plastic bowls and spoons. Walker picked up the icy-cold freezer can of vanilla ice cream and a big spoon to use as a dipper, then followed her out.

He didn't have another chance to talk to her until everyone had left except Clay and Shelby. Shelby and Jen stood at the sink, rinsing and loading dishes into the dishwasher, while Clay worked outside, putting away the folding chairs.

When Shelby pulled the ice cream canister across the

counter toward her, Walker saw his chance. He moved up beside her and nudged her with his elbow. "I can get this. You and Clay don't have to stay and clean up."

"We don't mind." Her curious gaze went from him to Jen then back. "I'll go help Clay with the chairs."

"Okay, thanks." As she left, Walker squirted dish-washing soap into the metal can. He glanced at Jen, who seemed engrossed in rinsing a glass baking pan. "Did you enjoy the party?"

"Yes." Even though her smile wasn't as bright as usual, it still put a kick in his blood. "Shelby was telling me how she and Clay were best friends for years before things turned romantic."

After passing the soaped-up can to Jen for rinsing, Walker reached for the meat platter. It was too big for the dishwasher so he washed it by hand. They worked in silence for a few minutes. A couple of times his arm brushed against the soft satin of hers.

As she began drying the canister, a memory flashed through Walker's mind and he chuckled.

"What's funny?" she asked.

"I was just thinking about the first time my wife made homemade ice cream."

"Oh?" Jen looked interested, so he continued.

"She forgot to put in the vanilla."

"Ugh."

"Yeah, it tasted pretty bad. She was so mad at herself. After that, she taped a big note to the ice cream freezer that said, 'Add Vanilla!'"

"You've never talked about her before," Jen said quietly.

He knew he hadn't. And he realized with some surprise this was the second good memory he'd had of his wife in the last two days. For the first time in two and a half years, his thoughts of Holly hadn't been of her or their baby dying. Of them being killed over a damn necklace.

Once the dishes were finished, Walker wiped down the dining table while Jen cleaned the countertops. He knew he needed to apologize.

He backed against the counter, hands curled over the edge as she rinsed out the dishrag. "Listen, I'm sorry about last night."

She looked at him, a small frown on her face.

"For snapping at you after we got back from the grocery store."

She shrugged. "It's okay."

"No, it's not. All you did was ask a question and I jumped down your throat. I'm sorry."

"Walker—"

"Those guys you asked me about in front of the shelter? One of them is an employee. I didn't recognize the other one."

She hesitated for a moment, looking uncertain. "They obviously bothered you in some way."

"Yes." He rubbed a hand across his nape, his arm brushing hers. "I figure you've heard by now that my wife and baby were murdered."

She felt herself go still on the inside. Her breathing shallowed. This was the opening she'd been waiting for. Maybe—just maybe—he'd give her information that would lead to her proving whether or not he was the Payback Killer. Just the thought had her hands going clammy.

She nodded.

"Ever since it happened, I've been trying to find out who killed them. The only information I have is that the man is homeless and has a scar across the knuckles of his right hand. So I check the homeless shelters regularly. When I saw the new arrival at Helping Hands last night, I forgot about everything else except talking to him and getting a look at his hand."

"Did you go over there and check him out?" She'd gotten a good look at the guy's face, so if he wound up dead, she would know it was the guy Walker was talking about.

"Yes. He didn't have scars and didn't know anyone with any on their right hand."

Relief rolled through her, but she couldn't stop. "If you'd seen scars on his hand, what would you have done?"

He stared at her for a long minute. "Called the police. What else?"

"I don't know. Faced with something like that, a lot of emotions come into play. Anger, for one. In your situation, I have no idea what I would do."

"What do you think?" She thought she saw a flash of hurt then his eyes narrowed. "I'd kill someone?"

"No!" She really, *really* hoped not. It was clear he wondered why she was pressing so hard. She laid a hand on his arm. "I wasn't trying to pry. You don't have to tell me all this."

"I know, but you're my partner and the way I treated you was wrong." He didn't think he'd talked about his investigation to anyone except Shep and his family, but he couldn't let this thing stay between him and Jen. "I'm not saying I won't get mad sometimes. Or intense. But I shouldn't have been a jerk."

She was quiet for a moment. "Thanks for telling me."

"You had a right to know."

"I'm glad I didn't do something inadvertently."

"You didn't." Those gorgeous eyes of hers just knocked him flat. Every time he was this close to her, his blood hummed. His gaze dipped to her soft, pink mouth, and he wanted another taste.

Talking about his wife's murder should've drowned any heat Walker felt for Jen, but it hadn't. If anything, it heightened his awareness of her. The damp curl behind her delicate ear. The petal softness of her skin. That flirty scent of hers. She had slowly been pulling him out of hibernation, and he wanted her with an intensity he couldn't remember ever having.

He shouldn't feel this way about her. He wasn't ready. At least, his brain wasn't. His body had been ready from "jump."

She licked her lips, and lust slammed into him like a fist. He wanted to kiss her again, wanted to lift her up onto the counter and get inside her.

Heat flashed in those stunning blue eyes and he knew she wanted it as much as he did. Her lashes fluttered down; her breath feathered against his mouth.

Just as he leaned in, she flattened a hand on his chest, stilling him. "No," she murmured.

His heart kicked hard. He closed his eyes and straightened. Her hand was still on him, burning through his T-shirt. He waited, his gaze locked on her face. She moved her fingers, almost stroking him, then bunched his shirt in her fist.

"We said we weren't going to do that again, and I don't think we should."

"I remember." His voice sounded rusty. His body was hard. He could practically taste the dark sweetness of her mouth. He covered her hand with his, holding her in place so she couldn't move. "I still want to."

Her pulse jumped in her throat. "It's a bad idea."

His body was throbbing. "Because we work together."

"Yes, plus...I'm not interested in getting involved."

"Okay." Well, that was pretty clear. And stung his pride enough that he looked pointedly down at her hand still on him.

She seemed to be having a hard time letting go of his shirt, but she finally uncurled her fist and released him. When she did, she backed up a step. "I'd better be going."

"Okay."

After saying goodbye to Shelby and Clay, Jen started for the front door and Walker followed.

As she started toward her Jeep, parked at the curb, he snagged her elbow. "Are we okay? I mean, about working together. Did I screw things up?"

"Because of last night?"

He nodded.

"No. Everyone has bad days, Walker."

"What about the kiss?"

A look he tagged as pure panic flared in her eyes. "What about it?"

"That isn't going to be a problem, is it?"

"Of course not." She smiled. "It's already forgotten."

He'd tried to forget it, and he couldn't. He didn't want her to, either. It might have been almost a week since that kiss at her apartment, but it still turned him inside out every time he thought about it.

She'd been just as affected as he had. He'd felt it in every line of her sleek body. He'd tasted it. He wanted to take her to the ground right now and kiss her until she admitted she hadn't forgotten a damn thing.

He *should* forget that kiss, but it wasn't going to happen.

She had been right to stop him, but as he watched her drive off, it didn't feel right at all.

Chapter 7

Jen had told Walker she'd already forgotten their kiss.

Two nights after the party at his house, she admitted that was one of the biggest lies she'd ever told in her life. She hadn't forgotten anything. She wanted to kiss him again. She wanted more than that. And another part of her—the smarter part—was screaming she should get away from him. But she *had* to work with him until she solved this case. She had reminded herself of that more than once yesterday while on duty.

So, late in the afternoon on their next day off, she was staking out his house with Detective Robin Daly in a non-descript dark compact.

The surveillance had been Jen's idea, and Robin had thought it a good one. Maybe because the detective believed Jen was hoping to catch Walker in the act of killing another victim. Secretly, Jen hoped there might be another murder with the same M.O. tonight, and she and Robin would be Walker's alibi.

Her heart said he wasn't the Payback Killer. She needed something concrete to prove it.

They had arrived about five-thirty at the fairly new gated community and driven the curving streets past a creek to the back of the addition. When they had seen Walker's silver SUV in his driveway, they had parked down the lush tree-lined block from his buff stone country-style house. Traffic had slowed considerably the last two hours.

She had already told Robin about the incident in front of the firehouse when Walker had become completely absorbed by the men in front of the homeless shelter.

"When I asked if he was okay, he said yes and didn't offer anything else." Jen didn't tell Robin he'd snapped at her. "But at the shift party, he explained that he regularly checks the homeless shelters for anyone matching the description of the man who killed his wife. Even though I already knew that, I thought it was good that he shared something."

Robin nodded.

Jen was surprised at what he'd shared, was surprised that he *had* shared at all about why he'd behaved the way he had. And the long pause when she'd asked what he would've done if the stranger had scarred knuckles had made her pulse skip. Had he said he would go to the police because it was the socially acceptable answer? Or because he was a law-abiding citizen?

She wanted him to be innocent and she couldn't allow herself to think that way. He was the primary suspect in a serial murder investigation. Her job was to report what she found or observed, period. Not hope for ways to clear him.

"I tried to snoop at his house during the party, but he caught me, so I said I was looking for the restroom."

"Did he buy it?"

Jen shrugged. "He appeared to. He was waiting on me in the kitchen when I returned, but he didn't say anything about finding me in the hall."

She didn't tell Robin that had been his first attempt at apologizing for snapping at her. She certainly didn't tell the other woman Walker had nearly kissed her. Or that Jen wished she'd let him.

Watching Walker's house, waiting to see if he went anywhere tonight, filled her with conflicting emotions. Determination to find the truth. Lingering hurt at the way he'd shut her out the other night. Uncertainty about how much to read into the fact that he'd explained why.

Once it became dark, Robin passed her a cup of coffee from the giant thermos she'd brought. Jen pushed a package of miniature peanut butter cups across the seat to the other woman. Their empty salad and fruit containers were stuffed in the restaurant's carryout bag.

Robin's shoulders were wedged in the corner of the door so she could read by the milky light streaming in from the street's floodlight.

Scanning her small notebook, the detective sipped her coffee. "Spencer and I went back over what we have on the Payback Killer's victims to see if we missed anything."

Jen's gaze stayed on Walker's silver SUV in the driveway. "Starting with the first victim?"

Robin nodded. "Do you know the background on any of them?"

"A little bit."

"Victim number one served seventeen years for murdering a little girl. Thanks to a computer glitch he was released, and two days later a twelve-year-old female was found dead outside Oklahoma City. His DNA was all over her, and a week after that he was dead."

"Hard to fault anybody for killing him." Any crime against children filled Jen with a red haze of fury. She knew it did the same to Robin and every cop Jen knew. "What about victim number two?"

"He was awaiting trial for a series of mailbox bombings and was released because of a technicality. About a month later, he was seen putting a pipe bomb in a mailbox. It exploded and severely injured an elderly woman. His burned body was found two days later."

Jen made a sound of disgust.

"Number three was the first one you worked," Robin said.

"Yeah, I remember the information you and Jack gave me about him. He was in prison for killing someone while driving under the influence. Within hours of his release, he killed a young married couple, again driving drunk, this time in a stolen car. He didn't have a scratch on him." She paused, tapping a fingernail against the steering wheel. "He was out about four months before the Payback Killer got him. Why wait so long?"

"Probably because the Payback Killer couldn't find him."

The tall, leafy trees up and down the street swayed in the wind. Jen's window was open slightly, and the scent of grass and car fuel mixed with the smell of coffee.

Robin flipped to the next page in her notebook. "The fourth victim was the meth dealer. He was convicted of making and selling drugs. A week after his release, he was making meth and selling it at schools."

"The Payback Killer is pretty much doing the world a favor." It was hard for Jen to judge the vigilante too harshly for ridding the world of murderers and drug dealers when she was trying to stop a killer, too. "Too bad it's against the law."

"No kidding." Robin set her coffee cup on the dash and made a note.

Jen's gaze scanned the partly wooded and rolling terrain of Walker's neighborhood. Moonlight spread across the hood of his SUV, the neatly clipped lawn and the trimmed hedges along the front of the house.

After unwrapping a peanut butter cup, she popped it in her mouth then smoothed out the foil wrapper. "Do you know yet when the most recent victim, the meth dealer, was released?"

"About six weeks ago."

"And killed less than a week after he got out," Jen mused.

"Right," the detective said. "There appears to be no pattern to when these murders are happening. So far, all the victims have in common is they've committed other serious, usually violent crimes after their release from prison."

Jen laid her head back against the seat.

Robin glanced at her watch. "It's almost midnight. Chances are good McClain won't leave his house tonight."

"Hopefully he won't. We're on duty in the morning and I'd rather not chase him around tonight."

"You have to report in about seven hours from now. If you want to nap for a bit, I don't mind watching on my own."

"I might take you up on that a little later. Right now, I'm too wired from the coffee."

Robin smiled, looking toward Walker's house. "I read a little about your last job in your file. You busted a prostitution ring in a firehouse?"

"Weird, huh? Sick, too."

"I would think it would be pretty difficult to find the facts, since it sounded like the male firefighters were the ones approached about participating."

"There were two female firefighters offering sex in exchange for overtime hours and sometimes just money. I got a break in the case when one of them asked if I wanted to make some extra money. When I said yes, she laid it out for me."

"Wow." Robin folded one leg under her. "Did people know you were a plant?"

"No. Not for sure. Speculation ran wild after the guys who operated the sex ring were arrested. There was never any proof, but several people treated me as if they suspected I was the one who'd busted the men involved."

"Did you stay in that firehouse?"

"For about two months. It was hell. I was glad to be sent to train as a SWAT medic with some guys from another station."

Robin studied her for a long moment. "I don't think I could do your job. I wouldn't want to, that's for sure."

"It isn't what I would choose, but I was assigned there." She usually didn't discuss her feelings about working for what was essentially the fire department's internal affairs division, but Robin was easy to talk to. "On my first case, I caught an arsonist-firefighter who'd been setting blazes for two years. I was sent in undercover after a family was killed in one of his fires. Discovering the torch was someone who the public trusted to protect them from the very thing he'd used as a weapon made me sick. Turning him over to the cops was a pleasure."

"Can't argue with that. And even though I don't care much for our IA division, I know they do some good, too."

"I *hate* having to lie to people, but the good results usually outweigh my conscience." *Usually,* she thought.

For the first time in her undercover career, she had doubts. "I didn't feel too bad about lying on those two cases, but other times I do."

"Does it bother you on this case?"

"Sometimes, even though I know I'm doing it for a good reason." She hadn't planned to confide in the other woman, but she found herself doing so anyway. "It troubles me more lying to Walker than it did with the others. Not just because he trusts me with his life as a firefighter, but also as a SWAT medic."

Robin nodded in understanding. "It would probably help if he weren't such a nice guy."

"It would help a lot."

Jen couldn't bear to think about how he was going to hate her if he found out what she was really doing in his fire-house. Why she spent as much time with him as she could.

"Ever gotten personally involved with a suspect?"

Jen's gaze cut to the other woman. Had she heard something in Jen's voice when she talked about Walker? "I can keep my feelings out of it. Sometimes it's difficult, but I've learned how."

Realizing she sounded defensive, she softened her tone. "Some days are worse than others. I try really hard to remember my job is to gather facts, not friends."

"That would be hard for me."

You have no idea, Jen thought vehemently.

"I mean, what if you got to be true friends with a suspect? Or romantically involved with one of them? That would suck."

"It would." It *did.*

"Has your job ever gotten in the way of a relationship? I know cops can't see their families or make contact a lot of times when they're undercover."

"I haven't had to deal with that in the three years I've been doing this job."

"You weren't seeing anyone before you left Tulsa?" Robin reached for the thermos and poured more coffee for both of them. "I'm a little surprised."

"I was engaged once, a long time ago, but it didn't work out. No relationship since then."

"That's something we have in common."

Jen took her fresh cup of coffee. "You've been engaged before?"

The detective's features tightened. "Yep, right up to the altar."

"What happened?"

"He dumped me at the very last minute."

"Was he a cop, too?"

"Yes, and a full-time jerk." Anger flashed in Robin's blue eyes.

"Why did he wait until the wedding?" Jen asked. "Surely he had doubts before. Were there any signs?"

"Not that I ever noticed. One of his groomsmen talked him out of marrying me."

Jen's jaw dropped. "A groomsman? I've never heard anything like that."

"It was hard for me to decide which one to shoot first. I'm glad I didn't marry the jerk, especially if his feelings were so weak that his mind could be changed that easily. But I sure don't appreciate other people butting into my business."

"No kidding! How long ago was that?"

"About five years."

It had been almost four since Jen had left Mark. Before she could ask another question, Robin's cell phone vibrated. The other woman checked the readout. "It's Detective Spencer," she said before answering. "Hello."

Glancing at Jen, Robin nodded. "Yes, she's here. I'm putting you on speaker." As she did so, she said to Jen, "He's not using the radio because he's away from his car."

After a moment, Jack's voice came over the line. "Can you hear me?"

"Yes," Jen and Robin said in unison.

"Good. About an hour ago I was called to a homicide, and at this point it looks like another Payback Killer murder."

"Well, we expected he'd kill someone else soon," Jen said.

"Yeah," Spencer said.

"Any guess about how long he's been dead?" Robin asked.

"The M.E. is here now. He needs more time to know for sure, but he thinks the guy might've been killed sometime in the last six hours."

Jen glanced at the detective beside her. "Well, one thing Robin and I can vouch for is that McClain has been home all night."

Which meant they could at least clear him for one murder. The relief Jen felt was so strong it made her chest ache.

Her gaze followed a white pickup as it approached from the end of the street. She frowned when it pulled up and parked at the curb in front of Walker's house. A tall, lean man got out and started across the lawn to Walker's front door.

Jen leaned forward, not yet able to see much detail. "Someone just showed up at McClain's."

"Who?"

"Not sure yet. Hang on."

As the man rounded the hood of the truck, light from a streetlamp coasted over a strongly planed jaw and dark, ragged hair. Recognizing the smooth, long-legged gait, a greasy knot formed in Jen's stomach. She went cold, then hot. *No, no, no.*

She cursed at the same time Robin drew in a sharp breath.

"Lawson?" Spencer asked. "What is it?"

"It's McClain!"

"What? Who? The guy who just showed up?"

"Yes," she said, her jaw clenching.

Robin muttered under her breath. "I know that pickup. It belongs to his brother."

"I thought Walker was at home." Jack sounded confused.

"So did we." Jen was swamped by a surge of frustration. This whole time, they had thought he was inside and they could give him an alibi for this latest murder. He hadn't been there at all.

She was still stewing about it on duty the next night. It was after nine-thirty, and the firehouse was quiet. Most of the guys were in the living area, watching TV. Walker had gone into the kitchen seconds earlier, so Jen followed.

Where had McClain been last night? What had he been doing? Why had he been driving his brother's pickup?

She wanted to ask him all those questions, but then she would have to reveal how she knew he hadn't been home. She could lie—*again*—and tell him she had dropped by his house for some reason, only to find he wasn't there. Or she could fish for information.

In the background, a football game blared from the television. Walker had just opened the refrigerator and glanced over his shoulder as she walked up. "Want something to drink? I'm having tea."

"That would be great. Thanks."

After filling two glasses, he handed her one and leaned his backside against the counter. He took a long drink and Jen couldn't look away from the strong column of his throat. A tuft of hair showed in the open vee of his uniform shirt, and she clamped down hard on the urge to unbutton it and run her hands over his deep, broad chest.

"Do anything exciting on our day off?" he asked.

Staked out your house for hours. "Nothing to talk about. What did you do?"

"Nothing worth mentioning."

Shoot. There was a growing impatience inside her, and a heavy disappointment. She and Robin had believed they had gotten a break in the case last night, but that hope had been shattered the instant Walker stepped out of the white pickup. Why couldn't he have been at home?

His dark, spicy scent slid into her lungs, tantalizingly male. She wanted to close her eyes and savor it.

The sharp trill of the phone snapped her out of her reverie. Walker dashed around the table and picked up the handset just as the phone rang again.

"Got it," he said to the person on the other end. Hanging up, he yelled, "Trouble at the shelter. Someone bring a medic kit!"

Jen reached the bay door seconds after he did. Shep, Farris and Shelby were a few steps behind her. She turned to relay Walker's instructions then kept going. She could see he was almost at Helping Hands.

By the time she reached the fairly new, dark green structure, he was at the front door, talking to a slender woman with a cap of dark curls. Jen came to a stop beside him in time to hear some of the woman's words.

"—afraid he's going to kill himself. He already hurt one of our volunteers."

"Where is he?" Walker asked.

"In a supply closet. He shut the door, but I can hear him talking to himself. He's very agitated."

"Did you call the police?"

"I told the nurse to do it after I called you guys."

"Good." Walker followed the woman inside. Jen went, too, spying the woman's name and title on the plastic tag pinned to her pale yellow shirt: Miriam Dozier, Assistant Director.

They went past a wide counter where visitors were greeted then continued down the hall.

"How badly injured was your volunteer?" Walker asked.

"A shallow, long cut across his chest. He's in the doctor's office." The director sounded calm, but concerned. "The volunteer said the man with the knife stabbed himself in the arm when he attacked and he's bleeding a lot."

Walker nodded. On their right was a laundry room with several pairs of stacked washers and dryers, a counter for folding clothes and a hanger rack.

Ms. Dozier stopped in front of a closed door marked Linen Supply. "He's in there. He locked the door after the volunteer ran out, then I heard a couple of clicks, so I'm not sure if it's locked or not."

From inside, they could hear repeated cries of "Stay away!" and "I'll kill you!"

A shiver rippled down Jen's spine.

Walker reached for the doorknob, and she grabbed his arm. "We should wait for the police."

"That guy could be bleeding to death. We need to find out."

"He's got a knife," Jen said calmly, although her grip tightened on Walker's arm.

Through the door, she caught mumblings—rapid, frenetic.

Hearing footsteps, she and Walker both looked back the way they'd come. Shep, Farris and Shelby strode down the hall toward them. Shep carried a medic kit.

Letting go of Walker's arm, Jen filled the others in on

what was happening. Heavy kicks rattled the wall at her back, accompanied by more shouting.

Shep frowned. "Maybe you should wait for the cops, McClain."

"Yeah," Farris seconded. "We don't have to go in there. I'm not going to."

Walker's jaw set and he held out his hand. Shep passed him the medic bag.

"Thanks." Walker knocked on the door. "Sir, can you hear me?"

"Get away!" the man bellowed. "Stay away!"

"Are you hurt, sir? Can you tell me that?"

"Yes, they cut me! They're trying to kill me!"

"I'm a paramedic. I can help you if you let me come in and look at your injury."

"No! You'll let them kill me!"

"I want to help you. Let me show you my medical bag."

The man argued for another minute. Jen's nerves coiled tighter and tighter. Finally, Walker convinced the man to let him come in. Trying the knob, he found the door unlocked and opened it about a foot. He set the black medic kit just inside.

"No guns!" the man screamed.

"No one has a weapon, sir," Walker said. "Just medical supplies."

Long seconds of silence ticked by. Jen and Walker exchanged worried looks.

"Okay, just you," he finally said in a weary voice.

Before Walker could move, Jen grabbed his hand. "There's no way you're going in there by yourself."

"You heard what he said."

"I don't care. You don't know the situation. I'm going with you."

"No, you're not." Walker's green eyes stayed on her, but he spoke to the firefighter behind her. "Shep, help me here."

"She's right, man. You shouldn't go in there alone."

"You can go with me."

"No," she said, before Shep could answer. "I'm your partner. And we're wasting time."

Walker scowled at her and she stared back, unflinching. She didn't care if it annoyed him. There was no way he was going into a dark place alone with some mentally unbalanced knife-wielding man.

"If I'd gotten here first," she said in a low voice, "you wouldn't let me go in alone. The longer we stand here arguing about it, the more blood he's losing."

Walker muttered something under his breath. She couldn't understand the words, but she got the gist. He didn't like it.

He finally asked the injured man, "Can my partner come in, too? I may need her help."

After a pause, the man agreed. Jen and Walker slowly, carefully, stepped inside. The long, narrow room was filled with rows of tall shelves.

"Shut the door!" the man yelled. "Shut it!"

By the light slanting in from the hallway, Jen caught sight of stacked towels and sheets. The man wore scuffed work boots and dirty jeans; his upper torso and face were in shadow. Blood pooled on the linoleum tile.

"Shut it!" he snapped.

As Walker closed the door, he reached for the light switch. "No!"

"Sir, I need light to see your injury."

"Flashlight," Jen breathed next to Walker's ear.

He nodded. "My partner has a flashlight. She's going to turn that on, all right?"

"Don't shine it in my face," he ordered. "They'll see me."

"She won't." Walker put his bag on the floor and pulled on a pair of gloves as he knelt next to the man. "May I look at your arm?"

Jen went to her knees, too, placing the flashlight on the floor so she could glove up. She held the light steady, shivering at the feral look in the injured man's eyes.

"What's your name?" Walker asked calmly, putting his hand on the man's arm.

"Arnie." His gaze was sharp, following Walker's every move.

The scent of fabric softener mixed with the strong odor of an unwashed body.

Walker examined the cut, which was just above the bend of the arm on the inside. "It would be easier for me to bandage your wound if you'd give me the knife."

"No! It's mine!" He jerked back, the knife swinging wildly toward Walker's face.

Jen flinched. She didn't see how Walker kept from doing the same.

He stayed calm and kept working on Arnie. "It's okay. Just be still and I can fix you right up."

"Bestill, bestill, bestill." Arnie ran the words together, saying them faster and faster. *"Bestill."*

Memories slammed into Jen—the mood swings, the paranoia, the fear. Suddenly there was a roaring in her ears and she fought to keep her hands steady.

Walker spoke quietly, "I'm going to clean the blood from your arm, okay?"

"O-okay." The man's voice shook; in the indirect beam of the flashlight, his skin looked waxy. "Don't hurt me. Please don't hurt me."

Jen felt Walker's slight pause at the man's abrupt shift in mood, the childlike plea. "I won't. I'll go easy."

She held her breath, although she wasn't sure if it was for herself or for Walker. Gently and systematically, he cleaned the wound. The patient's gaze darted between him and Jen, and he whimpered.

Walker spoke softly, "You've got a pretty deep cut here, Arnie. It may need stitches—"

"No!" the man snarled. His eyes were frenzied and his face glowed with a sheen of sweat. "Don't touch me! I'll kill you!"

The man's erratic behavior put a hard knot in Jen's stomach. Her head started to pound. She knew what this was. Her chest closed up; she couldn't breathe.

"I'm not going to hurt you," Walker soothed. "I won't stitch you up, just bandage your arm and make it stop bleeding. Will you let me do that?"

The part of Jen that wasn't fighting off the past admired the way Walker handled the patient. He remained steady. Jen had to do the same.

Focus. She tightened her grip on the flashlight, realizing her hands were clammy. A large patch of blood stained Walker's uniform shirt.

"You want to help me?" the patient asked in a small, shaky voice.

The man's extreme emotional shifts had Jen swallowing hard, throat tight.

"Have you seen the people who are trying to kill me? Do you know where they are?"

"They aren't here, Arnie. The only people here are people who want to help you. Me and Jen."

The man nodded, his gaze wary and troubled as he stared at Jen.

Recognizing the delusions and paranoia as signs of a manic episode, her heart felt like it cracked open. A suffocating heaviness settled over her. *Stay in the moment,* she told herself, fighting off the vicious black memories churning inside her.

Walker looked over and said something to her. She realized he wanted an ABD and slowly reached into the medic bag for one.

Remembering how noise sometimes pushed Mark from a state of calm into a frenzy, she tried to be as quiet and careful as possible. Her hand closed around the pressure bandage and she leaned forward to give it to her partner.

At her movement, the man screamed and lunged toward Walker. The knife's blade glinted dully in the shadowy light as it sliced past his face. Jen's heart nearly stopped. She moved a second after Walker, who managed to grab Arnie's wrist and twist it until the weapon thudded to the floor.

Jen grabbed the handle and pulled the knife toward her, then shoved it to the far corner. She heard it slide across the room as she turned back to help Walker. Suddenly Arnie curled up in a ball and started to cry.

Looking completely stupefied, Walker stared down at the man.

All the horror from Jen's years with Mark swelled up like acid. Tears stung her eyes. It took everything she had not to run out of the closet. Beneath the smells of unwashed flesh, antiseptic and blood, Jen caught a faint dark spice. Walker.

His scent kept her steady as she struggled to level out her breathing. She managed to put her emotions aside and do what had to be done.

Walker quickly wrapped the pressure bandage around the man's arm, speaking calmly, "You're going to be okay, Arnie."

The man continued to sob, a steady hiccuping moan that

stripped Jen's nerves raw. The room closed in and she couldn't get enough air. Panic flared.

"I'm opening the door," she said, her voice thin and reedy.

"Wait." Walker finished the bandage then patted the patient's shoulder. "Arnie, will you let us take you out of here? Get you cleaned up?"

The man replied, but Jen couldn't understand his words. When Walker nodded at her, she opened the door slowly and held up a hand to stay the people gathered in the hall outside.

Ms. Dozier stood there with two police officers, a short, thin man wearing a blood-stained shirt who Jen decided was the injured volunteer, a woman whose name tag identified her as a doctor and the firefighters from Station Three. Captain Yearwood was also here now.

Arnie was still in the fetal position. Walker motioned Shep and Farris inside, explaining to the patient that the other men were going to pick him up. The man stared at them, unresponsive when they carried him to a gurney in the hall.

Walker stepped out, glancing at the doctor who was directing the firefighters down the hall to the health care clinic. "Does anyone know who he is?"

"I spoke to a caseworker at Griffin Memorial." Director Dozier named the Oklahoma City hospital that helped a lot of the homeless mentally ill. "They know him. He had a waiver on file so they were able to give our doctor the list of his medications. She's already started Arnie back on them."

Jen was grimly familiar with the problems that came from someone not taking their meds, the heartbreaking cycle. Take them and feel nothing. Don't take them and hurt yourself, as well as the people you love.

After the officers questioned Jen and Walker, they moved

on to the director. The woman declined to press charges, saying the mentally ill needed to feel they could still come here. Even though the wounded volunteer also decided not to press charges, the officers had no choice but to arrest Arnie for armed assault and take him into custody. Leaving the shelter, they transported him to a mental holding facility inside St. Anthony's Hospital.

Ms. Dozier accompanied the firefighters to the front entrance.

"Thank you so much." She shook Walker's and Jen's hands, then looked around the group of people. "All of you. I don't know what I would've done. He would never have let me come in there."

"You're welcome," they all said.

As the firefighters made their way back to the firehouse, Jen felt as though she were walking through a thick batting. The night felt stagnant. Colors were dim; sounds were muffled. And at the same time, adrenaline zipped through her system, shocking her nerves into near-numbness.

Once back in the firehouse, she managed to keep her thoughts on Walker and how he'd handled the situation. Calm, compassionate. One realization kept circling back to her. He had risked his life to help a violent homeless man.

At the time, Walker hadn't known the man was violent due to mental illness and not because of any criminal tendencies. Arnie had used his knife on a volunteer and on himself. Dangerous was dangerous, no matter the reason.

Why would Walker help someone like that if he were the Payback Killer? If he were going to turn around and kill another violent homeless man? It didn't compute. He hadn't hesitated to go in alone, which still sent a stab of cold fear through her. Thank goodness she'd been there.

He could have been hurt or killed. Now that the adrenaline was ebbing, that possibility hit Jen all over again. Combined with the unexpected ambush of memories, she felt her control start to unravel.

She tried to keep herself together as she followed everyone into the kitchen, staying slightly outside the loose circle they formed around the dining table. The others kept asking Walker questions about the patient's erratic behavior, speculating as to whether the man had been high on drugs or if he was really mentally ill.

Why couldn't everyone just shut up? Jen had lived with mental illness, and she knew the signs Arnie exhibited were indicative of a severe mood disorder, maybe bipolar disorder.

She felt raw, split open, and the walls pressed in on her. Her restraint snapped and she turned blindly for the door. She had to get out of there.

Chapter 8

One minute Jen was in the kitchen with everyone, the next minute she was gone. Walker felt her leave then turned to confirm it.

She had been acting edgy since they'd finished with Arnie, and Walker had assumed it was due to an adrenaline crash, coming down from the high that resulted after rescuing people. Now, he didn't think so.

Going after her, he walked out of the firehouse and looked over the well-lit property, scanned the distance between the driveway and the shelter, then the street. When he didn't see her anywhere, he headed for the back of the building and the parking lot. The floodlight mounted on the telephone pole behind the station threw off plenty of light for him to see where he was going.

He felt super-energized, as usual after a harrowing rescue or a fire, but the rush was ebbing. He rounded the corner of the firehouse and stepped off the curb, moving along the west-facing row of parking spaces. His rubber-soled shoes were quiet on the asphalt. Milky-white light spilled across the small lot, and he saw Jen standing motionless against the door of her Jeep, her back to him, her head bent. At the sight of her, a tension in his chest eased.

Walker covered the distance between them until he stood a couple of feet away. His SUV was on one side of her vehicle, and Shep's Viper was on the other. Light slid into shadow, polishing her skin to a lustrous sheen. He thought she probably would've heard him coming, but when she didn't look over her shoulder, he asked, "Are you okay?"

She jumped, grabbing for the door and snatching it open. "Just came out to get some things."

She leaned into the vehicle and reached for something. He thought he saw her swipe at her cheek. When she straightened, she held up a white plastic shopping bag. "Refills for my soap and shampoo."

He wondered which of those was responsible for the musky floral scent that teased him every time he got close to her.

"I'll be right in." Her voice was tight, controlled. Too controlled.

And she wouldn't face him. He moved closer, curling a hand over the top of the door at her back. "Lawson, is everything all right?"

"Sure." Her voice was bright with false reassurance. "Why wouldn't it be?"

"Are you jittery because the guy held a knife on us?"

"A little." She turned, giving him a wobbly smile, but she wouldn't meet his eyes. "But I'm fine."

"You're not fine." He stepped around until he stood in the vee of the open door with her. Close enough to feel her warmth. And the tension pulsing off her in waves.

She shifted uneasily. "Shouldn't we get back inside?"

"We can take a minute." His gaze roamed over her face and when she finally looked at him, he frowned at the stormy emotion in her eyes.

In the pale light, he thought he saw a damp streak on her cheek. He reached up and rubbed it lightly with his thumb. "Have you been crying?"

"No."

She answered so fast he knew she was lying. He lowered his arm. "What's going on, Jen?"

"I told you, noth—"

"Something's bothering you. Is it about our call-out?" He braced one hand on the door by her shoulder, the other on the roof, caging her in. "Tell me what it is."

She shrugged. "The rescue was intense. I just needed a little downtime."

He might have believed her except for the haunted look in her eyes and the stranglehold she had on the plastic bag. What the hell? "There's more. What is it?"

"He almost stabbed you!" The words burst out of her. "What if I hadn't gone in the closet with you? Do you realize how risky that would've been?"

It sounded like… "Are you *mad* at me?" he asked in disbelief.

"No—Yes. No." She closed her eyes briefly. "I'm not mad."

She had been afraid for him, Walker realized. He'd been afraid for her, too. That was why he had argued with her about getting up close and personal with the volatile patient. But those kinds of situations were part of their job. "Somebody had to check the guy."

"The cops were on their way. The director said so."

"We had to know how much Arnie was bleeding. We couldn't wait."

"What's the rule? Two in, two out. Bad, McClain. Very bad."

"It wasn't a blaze, Lawson. We didn't have to follow fire procedure."

"I don't care. You should've had backup."

"I did," he reminded pointedly.

"That man was dangerous. Out of his mind." Her voice cracked. "There's no telling what he might've done."

Walker hadn't realized how apprehensive she had been during those minutes with the knife-wielding patient. He moved his hand from the Jeep's roof, nudged her chin up with his knuckle so that her eyes met his. "He upset you."

"Not him specifically." The tears welling in her eyes took Walker aback. "I…I knew someone like that once."

"Mentally ill?"

"Yes." She gave a choked laugh, dabbing at her eyes. "I didn't expect this to happen. His behavior brought up a lot of memories."

"Obviously not good ones."

"No, and they took me completely off guard."

His hand dropped to her waist. He waited.

"My fiancé, Mark, had bipolar disorder."

Walker's gut hollowed out. His thumb made slow, small circles above her waistband. "That had to be really difficult."

"His last year of law school, he started showing signs. He became impatient, short-tempered, mean. At first, we blamed it on stress and his heavy workload, but it kept getting worse, his moods more erratic, more extreme. One minute, he would be witty and sweet. The next, he would explode and throw things, hit…things."

"You?" Walker's hand flexed on her taut flesh. "Did he hit *you?*"

"No. He never hit anyone, just walls, doors, once a mirror." She exhaled a shaky breath. "His family and I finally convinced him to go to the doctor. He agreed because he knew something was wrong."

"That's when he was diagnosed." With his free hand, Walker pried the plastic bag out of her clenched fist and set it on the ground.

She nodded. "The doctor quickly found a combination of medications that helped, but Mark said he felt like a zombie. He couldn't focus or complete a thought. And he couldn't, we couldn't—" her gaze skittered away "—have sex. After he started the meds, he never wanted to, and on the rare occasion when he did, he couldn't do anything about it."

"Damn." The man must have felt completely emasculated. That would've made a bad situation even worse. "So, he stopped taking the drugs."

"Yes. The first time, he told me and his family that he'd done it, but they were so upset, he promised to start taking them again. He did for a little while." Her voice turned pensive. "His personality was so different on the medication. Grim, brooding. We went to counseling, but the whole situation took its toll."

As it had on Jen, too, Walker deduced.

"He blamed himself for everything. Being sick, doing his job poorly, for feeling like I was the only one holding us together. I didn't feel that way, but he did. He never had any energy and his sex drive was nil, so he stopped his meds again. He would disappear for days at a time then return filthy and having lost weight. Sometimes he didn't remember where he'd been. And," she choked out, "he thought I was trying to hurt him."

No wonder Jen had been emotionally steamrollered during their call-out.

Walker realized that at some point he had moved both hands to bracket her waist. He flattened one palm against the small of her back and urged her closer to him. "That had to be brutal."

She nodded, her hands on his biceps, fingering his shirt sleeves.

"So, what happened? I know you didn't get married."

"I couldn't handle never knowing where he was or if he was even alive. And I couldn't bear it that he thought I would hurt him. It was like he didn't know me at all." She took a deep breath, her breasts brushing his chest. "His family blamed me for his going off his meds. They said I must have been putting pressure on him about our relationship. That he stopped taking his medication because I made him feel bad for not being able to make love."

"That's bull."

"Their accusations came from fear and pain."

"That's no excuse for putting it on you." Anger flared at how those people had hurt her. Like she hadn't gone through enough hell by feeling she had abandoned the man.

"I stayed with him for a while even after I realized there was nothing left of the person I'd fallen in love with. Nothing left of us. Finally, I couldn't do it anymore and I walked away."

"And you still feel guilty about it, even though you know without a doubt you did everything you could."

She bit her lower lip, nodding. "Sometimes."

He was all too familiar with how blame bored in. His own guilt hadn't been caused by his failing to save the baby and Holly, but because he felt as if he were being unfaithful to her if he wanted another woman. It hadn't been an issue until he met Jen.

She stood quietly against him, her sweet-smelling hair

tickling the underside of his jaw. The teasing puffs of her breath against his throat had his pulse going ragged. It didn't matter that this was the most inappropriate time for him to be turned on. As close as they were, she had to feel his arousal, but she stayed in place.

It would be so easy to kiss her. That wasn't what she needed and yet he couldn't help brushing his lips against her temple.

She pulled back slightly, a vulnerability in her eyes that brought every protective instinct in him to life. "I didn't mean to go into all that. I thought I had put it behind me for the most part, but the situation tonight totally ambushed me."

"The past does that sometimes." He sensed that she, like he, hardly ever talked about what had to be one of the most painful things in her life. "I'm glad you told me about him."

"I used to wonder how things would've been for us if Mark hadn't gotten sick. Or if I'd stayed longer, but that was emotional torture. After a while, I had to move on."

"It was time." It was time for him, too, Walker thought. Since he had met Jen, good memories had taken the place of bad ones. He rubbed the small of her back. "You did the right thing."

"Most of the time, I think so."

"Are you still in love with him?"

"Not *in love,*" she said. "I do love him or maybe I love what we used to be. Does that make sense?"

"Yes."

Her gaze lifted to his, her blue eyes completely unguarded. "Are you still in love with your wife?"

Was he? He thought about his and Holly's wedding album, left on a coffee table in his living room so he could go through it whenever he wanted. In the past, that had been every night he was home.

It hit him then that he hadn't looked at it since the night

he'd kissed Jen. "I love her as part of who I was. Does *that* make sense?"

"Yes," she said softly. She smiled up at him and Walker's hold on her tightened.

Heat flared in her eyes and her gaze dropped to his mouth. Tension snapped tight between them. The urge to kiss her swept over him like a tide. He wasn't going to, but if she wanted to kiss him, he had no problem with it.

For one achingly long second, he thought maybe… Then the moment was gone.

Giving a shaky laugh, she rested a hand on his chest. "I'm so relieved Arnie didn't hurt you."

The concern in her voice reached deep inside him, got to that dark, empty place she'd touched the first time he'd seen her. He said gruffly, "Back at ya."

"So you aren't ready to trade me in for another partner?"

"Hmm, is that an option?" he teased, aching clear to his bones for her.

"Hey!" She lightly smacked him.

"I guess I'll give you another chance."

"Thank you *so* much," she drawled.

He grinned. Her eyes were liquid blue in the dim light. She was gorgeous.

He was awed by how long she had stayed with her ex. That situation must have seemed infinitely painful and lonely, felt like a slow, endless deathwatch. At least Walker had known losing Holly and the baby was final.

His gaze roamed over Jen's delicate features. He didn't only want her; he liked her. And admired her, he admitted. Something big and hot and scary unfolded in his chest.

Whatever she saw on his face had her drawing away, looking self-conscious. "Thanks for letting me cry on your shoulder."

"No problem." She could cry on him anytime she wanted. His shoulder, his chest, any part of his body. He eased back so she could close the Jeep's door.

After he scooped up her plastic bag, they started inside. What he felt for her was deeper than just care and concern for a work partner. A lot deeper. He thought maybe her feelings were changing, too. He didn't know if she would do anything about it and he wasn't sure if he should, either.

The next afternoon during firearms training with the SWAT team, Jen was still thinking about how sweet Walker had been the night before. Though he'd listened and asked a few questions, he mainly let her talk about Mark.

But for the rest of their shift, Walker had been really quiet, enough so that she had been surprised when he asked if she wanted to ride with him later to the shooting range. Not willing to miss an opportunity to stick close to him, she had said yes. The trip over had been comfortable, but again he'd been quiet.

The night before, she'd shared something she rarely discussed with friends, let alone a suspect. A lot of people were uncomfortable talking about mental disorders.

She had a brief moment of paranoia, wondering if his reserve might be because he suspected her of spying on him. She didn't think so, despite the fact she had lied to him only minutes earlier. Just after they reached the training center, she had slipped away under the guise of returning to his SUV for new batteries for her walkie-talkie.

Once there, she searched his vehicle. Just as with his locker at the firehouse, she found nothing to link him to the Payback killings. This time, she'd been more relieved than frustrated.

For a couple of hours, the team practiced rapid-fire sequences and shooting on the move. Inman called a water break and everyone walked to the van, which was parked by a chain-link fence at the edge of the shooting range.

First to reach the vehicle, Jen opened its back door. A large blue-and-white cooler full of ice sat between the facing bench seats that ran along the walls of the van. A sturdy iron rack, fashioned like a pegboard, stretched the width of the driver's and passenger's seats. Entry tools like battering rams and bolt cutters hung there along with extra weapons and ammo, several sets of flex cuffs, and some medical and electronic surveillance equipment.

Inman reached for the cooler, accidentally bumping a helmet off the end of one of the seats.

Jen caught the headpiece as it rolled toward her. "Got it."

"Thanks." He passed cold bottles of water from the ice chest to the team members, who stood talking in small groups.

Jen started to toss the helmet on the seat closest to her when she saw a small photograph tucked under the inside lip. Faded and wrinkled, it was of a blond-haired girl who Jen judged to be about twelve or thirteen.

"My sister," Inman said when he saw her looking at it.

"She's cute." Jen returned the helmet to the seat. It wasn't uncommon for firefighters to keep pictures of loved ones there. For a long time after she and Mark had split, she had carried a picture of him in her helmet. "She looks young."

"At the time of that picture, she was twelve."

"Does she live around here?"

"No. She passed away shortly after the photograph was taken."

"I'm sorry."

Taking a long drink of water, he looked off in the distance. "It was a long time ago."

Jen knew that didn't mean you missed the person any less.

Several minutes later, he called everyone back to the range to set up new targets. Jen and the others loaded their rifles as Inman indicated the paper head and chest silhouette targets tacked to irregularly spaced fence posts. "We're practicing hostage shots. I want you in teams of three."

The hostage shot was one that had to be perfect 100 percent of the time.

A hand-drawn outline of another head was slightly visible behind the front head target, the way it would look if a suspect used someone as a shield. Not only was the shooting area very small, the team had to be able to move fast and hit the mark dead-on every time. It took thousands of rounds of practice shots.

Inman had assigned a SWAT medic to each team, so she and Walker were in different groups, but that didn't mean she was any less aware of him. At least this way, she could observe him while keeping some distance.

He was still subdued, and she was starting to wonder if she'd gotten too personal with him the night before. For the first time since walking away from her fiancé, Jen hadn't felt alone. She didn't want to examine that too closely.

During the training session, there was the usual joking and bragging among the team members about who was the best shot. Twice, she felt Walker's gaze on her and when she looked at him, he kept his attention on her. A navy Presley Fire Department ball cap shaded his eyes from the afternoon sun so she could read nothing on his face. What was he thinking about?

It was nearly dark when Inman dismissed the team. Jen's nerves were stretched taut. She made sure her rifle was unloaded then placed it in the backseat of Walker's SUV with the duffel bag containing her vest, Taser and other equipment. When she turned to get in, he was there, holding the passenger door open.

"Thanks."

"You're welcome." He briefly touched her elbow to help her inside.

He closed the door and jogged around to the driver's side, sliding behind the wheel. After tossing his ball cap into the back, he reversed out of the parking space.

As he drove them back to her apartment, he was still trying to decide if he should ask her out. He'd been thinking about it a lot since the night before. Since their kiss, really, he admitted.

The SUV's air conditioner hummed quietly; her skin-warmed scent fluttered around him. When she rested her head on the seat back, he glanced over.

"Did you get any sleep this morning after the shift?"

"About four hours," she answered.

"That's good. After last night, I wasn't sure how you'd do."

Her drowsy smile turned her eyes soft and wanting, had him wanting to reach for her. "Afraid you might have to keep me awake today?"

He wouldn't have minded. He had a few ideas how to do it, and he might even come up with one that didn't involve getting her naked. After what she had told him about her ex, Walker had felt an increasing urge to protect her. Claim her.

She might still consider them only partners, but there was more to it for him, more than what he'd been willing to admit before. More than lust, although that was certainly part of it.

He hadn't forgotten the dark sweetness of her mouth, and he wanted another taste. Last night, he had thought she might give him one.

As Alan Jackson sang on the radio about a woman named

Dallas in Tennessee, Walker turned down the volume. "What you told me last night was amazing."

"About Mark?" There was a wariness in her voice.

"About how you stayed and tried to make it work. Not many people would've kept trying."

She looked at him. "You would have."

That look lit up every part of him. How did she get to him so fast, so completely? "Have you been in a relationship with anyone since then?"

"No. I've dated, but no one seriously."

"How long has it been?"

"Four years."

"That's quite a while."

She shrugged. "I've gone out, but never with anyone more than once or twice."

"I haven't dated at all."

"Two and a half years isn't that long to some people."

"It feels long enough to me," he murmured.

She tilted her head, looking curious.

Cars whooshed by as they moved through wide arcs of light from the streetlamps. Walker dragged a hand across his nape. "Since my wife died, I haven't even been interested in another woman. But you changed that."

She sat up, slowly. Surprise flashed across her face.

He was going for it. "The other night you said you'd forgotten about our kiss, but I haven't. I haven't been able to stop thinking about it and I don't want to. I don't want *you* to."

Emotion swam in her eyes. "We agreed—"

"No mixing personal with business. I know."

"Right."

He turned at the major intersection nearest her apartment complex. "I want to spend time with you, outside of work."

Her smile looked forced as she said lightly, "You don't think we're already attached at the hip?"

"No. Not yet anyway." His voice lowered suggestively. He liked the way her eyes went wide.

"Don't you think Captain Yearwood would object?"

"Not as long as we don't flaunt it at the firehouse." Desire, then wariness, flickered across her features. What was going through her mind? "Can you tell me you haven't thought about our kiss?"

She shifted uneasily in her seat.

"We almost did it again the other night."

"I remember." Her gaze went to his mouth, causing his muscles to tighten. He wanted to kiss her right now.

She laced and unlaced her fingers. "It doesn't seem like a very good idea."

"Because we work together?" He didn't ask if she was interested, because he knew she was.

She looked everywhere but at him, as though she were flustered by the idea of dating him. His partner, who could treat a wounded bleeding man in the dark, with gunfire raging around them. Walker couldn't believe it.

"I wasn't sure at first, either," he said. "Partly because of the job, and partly because I didn't think I should want you, but I've come to terms with that. I'd really like to see you."

"How am I supposed to say no when you tell me things like that?"

"You're not. At least, I hope you can't."

"I don't know."

"You're interested." He pulled into her complex and parked at the first available spot close to her unit, several spaces away from her Jeep. "If you aren't, tell me and I'll back off. Completely." For now. Maybe.

"What do you mean, completely?"

"I won't bug you about it anymore."

"Will it affect our working relationship?"

He stared out the window, considering. "I'd like to say no, but I'm not sure. I want you bad and I don't know if I can keep things the way they are now."

Turmoil darkened her eyes. "I don't want you to back off."

He let out a slow breath. "So you'll go out with me?"

After a long moment, she nodded.

"Good. How about tomorrow night? My brother and sister-in-law invited me to dinner, but I'll cancel."

"No," she said quickly. "Don't do that."

"But I want to see you."

"I don't mind going there."

"You won't feel weird? It'll be our first date."

"Would I be crashing your dinner?"

"No. In fact, you'd be helping me out. I'm under standing orders from my sister-in-law to bring a date anytime. I can't face Kiley alone. She's a cop." He gave an exaggerated shudder. "She carries a gun."

Jen chuckled. Looking thoughtful, she tapped a finger against her lips. "Will you be taking your homemade ice cream?"

He laughed. "Would it be a deal-breaker if I don't?"

"Yes."

"Then absolutely."

"Well...I guess I can't turn that down."

Walker grinned, elated and feeling slightly ridiculous about it. It was just a date, for crying out loud. "Good."

"What should I wear?"

"Nothing—" he chuckled when her mouth dropped open "—fancy."

"Okay."

He wanted to seal the deal with a kiss, but she had only just agreed to go out with him, and he didn't want to lose ground. "I better get you out of here before you change your mind."

He stepped out of the SUV and met her at the back, raising the cargo door, then hefting her duffel bag to carry it to her Jeep. She followed, holding her M-16 barrel-down against her leg. After Walker stowed her gear in her vehicle, they started up the stone steps to her apartment.

A shadow crossed her face. "Are you sure your brother and sister-in-law will be okay with this?"

"They'll be more than okay with it, trust me," Walker said dryly, just imagining their reactions. But the more he thought about it, the more he didn't want to share Jen on their first date. "Hey, let's go somewhere else."

"No," she said quickly. "Let's go to your brother's. I'm looking forward to it."

He searched her eyes. "You're sure?"

"Yes. I liked Collier when I met him. I'm sure I'll like his wife, too."

"Okay." He cupped her elbow as they rounded the corner of the stair railing. A few steps later, they came to a stop in front of her door.

The small fixture overhead put off a yellow-white light, gliding across Jen's face, making her skin look like velvet. "I'll pick you up. How does seven sound?"

"That's fine."

He grazed a knuckle down her cheek. "I promise I won't spring my family on you all at once."

Her heart squeezed. This would probably be the only time she would meet any of his family, and she'd be lying to them, too. Before, she couldn't have imagined it would be possible for Walker to hate her even more after learning the truth, but this would do it.

She unlocked her apartment door and turned the knob, caught by the heated pleasure burning in Walker's eyes. "See you tomorrow."

"For sure," he said in a deep silky drawl that shot sensation straight to her toes.

She watched as he walked down the steps, admiring the wide shoulders, the rangy muscular build. When he drove out of the parking lot, she could still feel his touch on her cheek.

He said he had tried to talk himself out of what was between them. So had she. She really had.

She shouldn't be going out with the man. She was *investigating* him. Good grief, she'd lied to him only hours ago so she could search his vehicle.

She had felt compelled to say yes to the date, especially when he had sworn to back off. She couldn't take that chance even though this was a dangerous line to walk. The frank male interest smoldering in his eyes ripped right through her defenses. Agreeing to have dinner with his brother and sister-in-law sounded safer than being alone with him.

She might be able to justify saying yes for all the right reasons, but she had also said yes for all the wrong ones.

Because she wanted to. She wanted *him*.

And she had realized he truly cared about her.

She cared about him, too. He had risked his life to help a violent homeless man. Why would he do that if he'd been going around killing other men like that? That wasn't the behavior of a killer, in Jen's opinion. And neither was the way he had cared enough to find her last night and ask what was wrong.

It was then she realized that deep in her heart, she knew he was innocent. He wasn't the Payback Killer. She knew that.

Now it was up to her to prove it.

Chapter 9

She had to be careful, Jen told herself the next evening as she and Walker arrived at his brother's charming thirties-style cottage. If she thought she'd been balancing on a tightrope between desire and duty before, she was toeing an even more tenuous line now that she'd agreed to go out with Walker.

He had picked her up early, but she didn't mind. If he hadn't, she would've changed clothes more than the three times she already had. In the end, she had worn a green-and-white floral sundress with a flirty, above-the-knee skirt paired with matching green sandals.

He wore jeans and a white shirt. On him, the clothes didn't look as plain as they sounded. Soft faded denim sleeked over a muscular backside, down the long length of strong thighs. His shirt cuffs were rolled back to reveal corded, hair-dusted forearms. The garment fit across his broad shoulders just right, hinting at the big biceps and rock-hard arms beneath, the muscular chest she'd felt for herself. Those dimples and the shadow of stubble on his jaw made him dangerous to her restraint.

His pager was clipped to the waistband of his jeans. Since he and Jen were the SWAT medics on call tonight, hers was in her purse.

His brother had offered to give her a tour of his home, and they started in the entryway. Walker rested a hand in the small of her back as Collier pointed to the brick floor, meticulously laid in a herringbone pattern. "This is a replica of the original."

"It looks amazing," she said. "Was it already here when you bought the house?"

"No. Walker and I put it down."

"Wow, I can't believe you did this yourselves!"

As Collier led the way into a cozy living room with a fireplace, Jen smiled at Walker. "You can fix cars, lay floors, put out fires. What else can you do?"

"Be happy to show you," he said in a low voice that sent a shiver through her.

Jen had forgotten how a first date felt with someone who caused that sweet tease of expectation, the butterflies of awareness with just a look.

They passed through the living area, the taupe carpet complementing a navy-and-burgundy plaid sofa and two navy leather recliners. From there, Collier took them down the hall off the living area that led to a full bath and three bedrooms. The khaki walls and white woodwork gave the house a clean look without being fussy.

Jen noticed a grouping of framed photos on one wall arranged around Kiley and Collier's wedding portrait. She smiled at her host. "I guess your wife didn't mind moving in here after you married. Your house is really nice."

A shadow crossed his face as he stepped into the master bedroom.

Tucking her hair behind her ear, she looked at Walker, wondering what she'd said.

He hooked her fingers with his, holding her back a second to whisper, "Kiley's house burned down when a suspect set off a gas bomb at her front door."

"How awful."

"When I first started as a fire investigator," Collier said, "Kiley and I worked a serial arson-murder case. Her house was torched when we closed in on the suspect's identity."

"Was she hurt?" Jen asked.

"Shot," he answered grimly.

"The suspect was killed," Walker added.

As his brother moved past a walk-in closet nearly the size of Jen's living room and to a door leading out to the patio, Walker said quietly, "She almost died."

Jen didn't know what to say. Filled with sympathy, she preceded him across the spacious room, asking about something less bleak. She glanced at Collier. "So, you met your wife while working a case?"

The big man nodded, opening the door and ushering them out to the patio.

They stepped onto a wide flagstone patio partially shaded by a vine-covered awning. Pots of red and gold mums clustered in threes put a finishing touch at the back of the house. A curving walkway of the same gray flagstone led down to a swing glider under a sprawling oak.

"This patio is gorgeous. Did you and Walker do this, too?"

"Yeah," Collier answered. "Just recently."

His red-haired wife rapped on the kitchen window that overlooked the backyard and motioned them inside for dinner. The food was delicious and the conversation easy. It was hard not to like Collier and Kiley McClain. They asked questions that showed interest but didn't make her uncomfortable.

After the meal, Jen rose to help clear the table. Walker went to the garage where he'd left his freezer of homemade ice cream. She smiled, thinking about how he'd teased her that the dessert was the only reason she'd agreed to go out with him.

Meeting the men on the patio, the women each carried two bowls of Kiley's blackberry cobbler topped with the frozen dessert. A slight breeze cooled the humid night and stirred the faint scent of berries and flowers. She also caught a whiff of Walker's clean male scent. They sat close enough that his elbow brushed her arm occasionally.

The atmosphere was relaxed and Jen enjoyed not only the conversation, but also watching the byplay between Walker and his brother. It brought back her old wish for a sibling, someone related by blood who she could feel close to.

After dessert was finished, she gathered everyone's dishes and took them into the kitchen. The room's white tiled countertops and navy striped walls combined with the modern appliances to bring the decades-old home up-to-date.

The men stayed outside, moving the table and chairs from under the awning back to the center of the patio. She began to rinse the bowls.

"Oh, no, no. Don't do that," Kiley said when she saw Jen. "You're my guest."

"You already did a ton of work by cooking. If I help clean up, it will get done much faster."

After a slight hesitation, the other woman nodded. "Okay, thanks."

Jen passed her a rinsed bowl and Kiley loaded it in the dishwasher.

They worked quietly for a minute before Jen said, "Collier told me you two met while working a case."

"Yes. It was a first case for both of us." Her voice turned soft. "I'd only made detective several months earlier, and Collier took over the fire investigator's duties right in the middle of the investigation after Terra Spencer went into early labor."

"I've met her," Jen said, recalling the titian-haired fire cop. "She seems really sharp."

"She is. And nice, to boot."

Collier opened the door and reached inside to pluck a kitchen towel from the counter.

"So, did you and Collier just decide one day you should go out?" Jen asked Kiley. "How did you get together?"

"She couldn't keep her hands off me," the big man quipped.

His wife rolled her eyes, taking a plate from Jen.

Jen smiled at the couple. "You started seeing each other while you were working the case?"

"Kiley didn't want to," he said, "but I wore her down."

The redhead grinned as she snagged another dish towel and snapped it against his jeans-clad leg. "Get out of here."

Collier hooked an arm around her neck and pulled her to him for a quick kiss, grinning as he went back outside.

Jen couldn't help comparing her and Walker's situation to his brother's. He and Jen may have met on the job, too, but their relationship would never reach the point of Collier and Kiley's. Even if Jen found something to prove Walker's innocence, he would still feel betrayed once he realized she had been spying on him, deceiving him and everyone else.

She rinsed a large pan, her gaze trailing out the window to him. Muscles flexed across his shoulders as he helped his brother fold up the giant patio umbrella. Anticipation hummed inside her.

A touch on her arm brought Jen's attention back to her hostess.

"Collier and I are so glad you came tonight. I hope it was all right that you were with us on your first date."

"It's been great." So great Jen was having a hard time keeping up her guard. "I've really enjoyed myself."

"So have we. I've seen Walker smile more tonight than I have in the last two years."

A knot lodged in her throat.

"Do you know about his wife and baby?"

Jen nodded, afraid her voice might crack if she answered.

"He's almost the guy he was when I first met him—light-hearted, fun, very engaging." Kiley glanced affectionately out the window at her brother-in-law. "That means the world to us. After Holly and the baby died, he just shut down. We were starting to fear he might never come out of it."

Perfect, Jen thought. Now she wouldn't only leave Walker feeling betrayed but also his family. The truth about Jen and her undercover investigation would come as news to Collier and Kiley, too. The only other people who knew about the covert operation were the two detectives who had been assigned to the case. Jen's heart clenched. "Walker and Collier seem to get along really well."

"They do. They're pretty close with their sister, too."

"Collier told me he and Walker laid the entryway floor and the flagstone."

"They only did the patio a couple of days ago."

That was the night Jen and Robin had staked out Walker's house.

"It took all afternoon and until about ten-thirty that night."

Ten-thirty? But Walker hadn't shown up at his house that night until after midnight.

"I'm surprised Walker wasn't dead on his feet," Jen said. "We had just come off a shift."

"They were both wiped out. Collier was too tired to even

drive Walker home. He just handed over the keys to his truck and we picked it up the next day."

So, where had Walker been between the time he left here and the time he arrived home?

Her thoughts were interrupted as he and his brother came inside.

Walker gave her a slow smile. "Ready to go?"

The frank male interest in his eyes set off a flurry of sensations in her stomach. Oh, boy. "If you are."

"Yep." He leaned down to hug his sister-in-law. "Dinner was great."

"Everything was wonderful," Jen said. "Thanks for having me."

"You're both welcome."

Walker's hand burned where it touched at the base of her spine as they walked out to his SUV. His brother and sister-in-law waved as Walker backed out of their driveway and started toward Jen's apartment.

Dusk had settled in sooty layers over Presley. Old-fashioned streetlights lent an antique charm to the city's streets. Walker reached over and took her hand, rubbing his thumb across her knuckles. "Did you have a good time?"

"I did. I like both of them."

"Thanks for keeping Kiley off my back."

"Yeah, she's really fierce." Jen laughed. "The entire night was fun. I'm glad our pagers didn't go off."

He nodded, asking her what she thought about him laying a flagstone walkway off his deck. Jen kept up her side of the conversation, but what she'd learned from Kiley about the time Walker had left her house the other night stayed in Jen's mind.

Detective Daly had let her know earlier the time of death for that night's Payback Killer victim. The M.E. had estimated it to be between 6:00 p.m. and 3:00 a.m. Plenty of time for Walker to have left his brother's house, murdered victim number four, then gone home.

The timing fit. It looked damning, but Jen didn't buy it. Staring at his lean features, the hint of a dimple, she just did not believe he was the vigilante she was searching for. So how was she going to prove it? She'd have to start back at the crime scenes, try to figure out if there was a reason why the killer had chosen those sites.

It seemed only seconds before Walker parked in front of her complex. "Do you want to keep the rest of this ice cream? There's not much left."

"Oh, yes. Thanks."

He got out and removed the metal canister from the wooden freezer tub where he'd repacked it to slow the melting. Once upstairs, Jen opened her apartment door so he could go in first. He set the can in her sink as she took down a large plastic container from a top cabinet.

After dishing the dessert into the bowl, she stored it in the freezer while he washed his hands at the kitchen sink. She stepped over next to him and bent to get a bottle of dishwashing soap from under the cabinet, squirting the liquid into the can.

Just as she turned on the water, Walker moved behind her and slid his arms around her waist.

Everything inside her went still. She breathed in his clean male scent, wanting to lean back into him, but she didn't. "What are you doing?" she asked lightly.

"Helping."

Helping mow down her last remaining defenses. "I'm practically finished."

"Mmm-hmm." He held her close, his face in her hair. The anticipation that had teased all night coiled inside her.

She washed the sticky container, then reached for the sink's hose. He put one hand on top of hers and flattened a palm low on her stomach, pulling her tighter into him as they directed the spray into the metal can.

Jen was burning up from the inside out. She knew she should either tell him to move or step away herself, but she couldn't make herself do it. He felt too good. His slightly rough palm covering her hand. His arms surrounding her. Her bottom nestled into his groin and the steel-hard feel of him, the warm spice of his dark, masculine scent had her wanting to turn and bury her face in his neck.

As they rinsed off the suds, he nuzzled his stubbled jaw against her cheek. Every nerve ending popped, and the heat she'd felt all night edged into need.

Nerves jangling, she set the canister upside down in the sink to dry and plucked a towel from the countertop. She swiped the cloth over Walker's hand and dried her own. "All done."

His teeth gently bit her earlobe, and sensation shot clear to her toes. She folded her arms over his so she wouldn't fall. "McClain!"

"Man, you smell good," he breathed against her neck, pressing hot kisses on her skin. Lifting her hair, he nibbled on her nape. "I just want to eat you up."

"Okay," she said dazedly. A faint voice warned she wasn't supposed to agree like that.

Obviously her idea of having the buffer of other people during their date hadn't worked so great. The anticipation of him finally touching her had only stoked the fire, and now she was a quivering mass of *yes*.

He cupped her shoulders, edging his fingers in under the wide straps of her sundress. His skin was hot and slightly raspy against hers.

He lightly traced her collarbone, grazing his lips against her temple, then her cheek, her jaw. He breathed in her ear, and any restraint she had went to dust.

She muttered his name and he made a rough sound, his hands going to her waist as he turned her toward him. He kissed her and she gave herself over to him, sliding her arms around his neck.

He tasted her, taking his time, pumping up that low throb already in her blood. A pulse beat hard between her legs. His tongue lazily played with hers and the room spun. He slid his hands into her hair as she caressed the strong column of his neck, the hard sinew of his shoulders. The feel of his arousal against her sparked a flare of impatience. His dark male scent made her crazy and she wanted to sink into it, sink into *him*. She couldn't get close enough.

She found herself sitting on the counter, her hands clutching biceps that were solid muscle. As he stepped between her legs, he pulled her right up against him in a way that had her entire body throbbing. She couldn't hold back a groan.

The sound had him moving his hot mouth to her jaw, down her throat. He was hard, blazing against her center as his tongue slipped under the vee of her bodice and licked the curve of her breast.

She pulled his head back to hers for a slow, deep kiss. His big callused hands cupped her calves then slowly slid around to her knees. As he smoothed his palms up the outside of her thighs, he pushed her skirt higher. The feel of his jeans against her bare skin had a delicious shiver moving through her.

She lost herself in the heated silk of his mouth, feeling his hands curve over her bottom and shift her so that his body hit hers at a higher angle.

A ragged moan spilled out of her, which had him gripping her even harder. She held on just as tightly, trying to steady her wildly rocking world. A humming started in her ears.

Walker lifted his head.

"No," she whispered. "Don't stop."

"Hang on." Breathing as hard as she was, his voice was husky. He rested his forehead against hers, color streaking his cheekbones, sultry intent in his eyes. He looked down and groaned.

Jen heard the sound again. Through a dreamy haze, she realized his pager was going off. Another buzzing noise came from the kitchen table where she had left her purse. Her pager was going off, too. Dispatch.

Due to the sensitive nature of information on SWAT callouts, the tactical medics were notified through a secured paging system. They would then meet at the firehouse and be given the location by a contact person there.

Curling one big hand over the top of her thigh, Walker pulled his phone from his jeans pocket and punched in a number. As he spoke to the person on the other end, he brushed his thumb back and forth on the sensitive skin high on the inside of her leg. She shivered, tightening her legs around him and feeling him surge against her.

"I'll let her know." Walker disconnected and slid his phone back into his pocket, his hand trailing up her inner thigh, making her squirm with need. "We've got a hostage situation."

Her senses were reeling. It was a good thing she hadn't tried to stand, because her legs felt like water. Still struggling to catch her breath, she stared blankly at him. "We have to go."

"Yeah."

His voice was gruff, the savage heat in his eyes sending a ripple of sensation through her. "I need to change clothes."

"Same here. I'll get your gear from the Jeep and come back up to change. We can go in my truck."

She nodded as he helped her down from the counter and walked with her into the small living room that boasted only a couch, TV and a oversized chair.

She turned toward the hall and her bedroom. "It'll only take me a minute."

He curled an arm around her waist and brought her to him, giving her a quick hard kiss. His eyes blazed down at her. "When the crisis is over, we're going to pick up where we left off."

She thought she nodded, but wasn't sure. She could hardly feel her body.

"See ya in a sec," he said, walking out the door.

She headed for her bedroom, struggling to process what they had just done. They had been *this close* to stripping off clothes. If they hadn't been interrupted, she had no doubt they would have. Jen couldn't have stopped herself, let alone Walker.

She stepped out of her shoes and unzipped her sundress, pushing it off. In a matter of seconds, she was dressed in black pants and a black medic T-shirt that declared in bold white letters: Even SWAT Dials 911.

Grabbing her boots to put on in Walker's SUV, she picked up her rifle and ammo, meeting him at the door. He wore the same black pants and T-shirt she did.

By the time they climbed inside his SUV, she had her legs under her. And her common sense was slowly surfacing. Their little makeout session had rattled her, excited her, but what knotted her up like a bad roller coaster ride was that it had never occurred to her to say no. Not once.

* * *

As they pulled out of her apartment complex, Walker's body actually hurt from need. He had cautioned himself all night not to move too fast because he didn't want to screw things up with Jen. He'd done fine until they had gotten back to her apartment, then he just couldn't keep his hands or his mouth off her any longer.

The taste of her cool sweetness still lingered, and he wanted to taste more of her. It was a struggle to dial back the hunger raking through him, but he did it.

As he maneuvered through town, Jen put on her socks and boots, then braided her hair. After she finished, she sat quietly, staring out the window. Streetlights threw enough light into the SUV to illuminate her face, the serious look there driving him crazy.

He might have thought she was just mentally preparing herself for what they might encounter, but he could feel her distancing herself from him. He wasn't having it.

"Did things move too fast in your apartment?"

A small frown creased her brow as she turned her head to look at him. "What do you mean?"

"I know I got kind of carried away up there. Maybe it was too much, too soon."

She studied him for a moment, then licked her lips. "It was probably good that we were interrupted."

"Why?" His hands tightened on the steering wheel. "You kissed me back. You seemed to be just as into it as I was."

"I was," she admitted.

"Then what's the problem? Are you sorry?"

"No. I'm just not sure it was a good idea."

"Oh, yes, it was. And I'll prove it to you after we resolve this standoff."

"Walker, I don't know if I'm ready for…more."

"My job is to get you ready."

Her eyes widened at his evocative words, but she said nothing.

He pulled up to the firehouse and they both went inside to learn the location of their call-out. Back in Walker's SUV, they headed for the east side of Presley's city limits and the home outside of town where a man was holding a couple hostage.

It took only a few minutes to reach the outskirts of Presley. After two miles, Walker turned south on a dirt road. The area became increasingly remote and quieter. No *whoosh* of nearby traffic, no overlap of car radios and voices and horns. Lights mounted on regularly spaced electric poles illuminated the rolling pastures and the thick brush scattered across the landscape.

As Jen checked her blow-out pack, then his, he continued the conversation they were having before they'd stopped at the firehouse. "Jen, I hear what you're saying about being uncertain and I won't push, but I want you. I want to put my hands on you right now."

Even in the poor light, he could see a flush darken her cheeks.

"I can take it slower. For a bit." His pulse had finally settled into a steady rhythm. "But I won't back off, unless that's what you want."

It was a long time before her gaze met his. "It isn't."

Walker drove up a grassy rise and pulled up under a massive elm tree. He killed the engine. "We'll talk again after this is over, okay?"

"Okay."

They joined Inman and the rest of the team at the SWAT van just down the road. The suspect was inside a small white frame house, which was visible across the dirt road and through the remote camera system. One of the first things the team set up during a call-out, the wireless camera on a tall tripod gave a three-hundred-sixty-degree view of the thickets and trees ringing the small dwelling. There were no other houses or people nearby.

Their team leader kept his voice pitched low. "The guy has two hostages, male and female. These cops have been out here for seven hours. When they called us, negotiations had broken down, then about five minutes ago, the male hostage ran out and the suspect shot him. The medics need to go get him."

Walker and Jen scanned the landscape for the closest cover and agreed on a dense thicket of cedar bushes and brush a hundred yards from the house. It would provide a good temporary refuge for the injured person, and they could carry any victim through the heavy woods behind the thicket. The team agreed to regroup at the van.

Inman touched his earpiece and listened. "Ten-four." He turned to the team. "Get in position at the edge of the property."

Tension vibrated in the still night air. The SWAT team silently moved across the dirt road and lined up behind a row of trees. Walker and Jen both put on a pair of gloves.

"Medic up!" Inman ordered.

Walker and Jen hustled to the center of the line and ducked behind two teammates with shields. Even though he and Jen were suited up and armed, their primary duty tonight was to provide immediate paramedic care to an injured team member or other victim. Behind the ballistic protection, they moved slowly forward.

Watery moonlight filtered through the trees and fanned out over the neglected yard, giving them enough light to see. They reached the injured hostage and knelt, Jen examining one side of the man's body and Walker the other. He found blood and one gunshot wound on the side of the man's neck, then managed to locate a thready pulse. Jen touched his hand, signaling there were no wounds on the other half of the man's body.

Right now, they cared about stopping the bleeding and keeping the victim breathing. Using a hemostatic agent to speed up clotting of the area, Walker sprinkled the special granular product onto the wound. It would act as a sponge to absorb the water from the blood and produce a stable clot. When he was satisfied the bleeding had stopped enough to move the patient, he tapped Jen's hand to indicate he was ready.

They each hooked a hand under the man's arm and began to drag him. The teammates providing cover kept pace with them until rapid gunfire erupted from the house. Tierney, who stood in front of Walker, went to his knees. His shield lowered for maybe a second, two at the most.

"I'm not hit," he yelled, pulling the protective covering back into place.

A shot whizzed past Walker's head, then another bored into the ground beside him. He and Jen hunkered down behind the other men.

Where was that damn gunfire coming from? A basement window, Walker pinpointed. Just then, something slammed into his chest with the force of a baseball bat. He fell back, pain erupting in his sternum. He'd been hit.

Chapter 10

Heart hammering, blood cold from seeing Walker go down, Jen kept moving as SWAT surrounded the house and entered. She got the patient out of the hot zone and released him to the paramedics, who then left immediately for the hospital, red and blue lights strobing in the night.

She headed straight to Walker. Where had he been hit? How badly? When she reached the cedar bush and saw him sitting up without assistance, talking to Inman, her relief was so sharp, so overwhelming, she couldn't get a full breath. Once their team leader finished, he strode across the road toward the police lieutenant on the scene.

The rural floodlight several yards away gave off enough light to show the blood that covered Walker's gloved hands and spattered his neck and arms. As she got closer, Jen realized she was shaking. Her throat tightened when he gave her a crooked grin.

Fighting off her reaction, she knelt and reached for him, then pulled back. Her gloved hands were still streaked with the hostage's blood. "Where are you hit?"

"My vest stopped the bullet." Grimacing, Walker touched the center of his chest.

"There's blood," she said unsteadily, spotting it on his bulletproof vest. "A lot of blood."

"I'm okay, Jen," he said softly. "None of it's mine."

"Good to know." A breath shuddered out of her. Seeing him fall had caused her brain to seize up. When he had croaked out, "Go, go, go!" she'd been able to keep moving only because of her training. Leaving him behind, not knowing how badly he was hurt, had torn a piece out of her.

When Walker had gone down, the situation had been quickly reevaluated. An imminent threat to life meant that SWAT took over. There was no more negotiation after that, just the necessary steps to resolve the situation as quickly as possible.

As the suspect was led out of the house in cuffs, Walker got to his feet. Jen matched his measured pace across the dirt road dappled with a mix of yellow light from the electric pole and pale silver from the moon. Once they reached the van to meet the rest of the team, she opened the vehicle's back door and urged him to sit.

He did, carefully unstrapping his vest. She tossed her soiled gloves into the biohazard receptacle under the seat and put on a fresh pair, then helped lift the protective garment over his head.

She stared at the blood-spattered Kevlar, feeling almost numb. "You sure you're okay?"

"Yeah." After discarding his gloves, he pulled up his black T-shirt, and Jen winced at the beginnings of a wicked-looking bruise in the center of his chest.

Hands trembling, she set his vest aside then handed him an alcohol-soaked pad. He cleaned the streaks of red from his neck and arms, used another pad to wipe his face.

"Thank goodness that blood isn't yours." She peeled off her newest pair of gloves and disposed of them.

Walker looked up at her. Whatever he saw in her face had him reaching for her hand and squeezing.

He let go as the other team members gathered around the van.

"McClain, how are you?" Inman asked.

"Just bruised."

"Glad to hear it isn't worse. The suspect is in custody and the female hostage is unharmed."

"What happened with Tierney?" Walker wanted to know why his teammate had stumbled.

"He stepped in a hole, but he's fine." Inman turned to Jen. "What about the injured hostage?"

"The paramedics will call after they talk to a doctor," she said.

The commander glanced around the group. "Where the hell was that guy shooting from?"

"A basement window." Walker shifted with a grimace.

"How did those rounds get past the shields?" Inman asked.

"One of them made it through when Tierney stumbled." Walker frowned. "I have no idea how he was able to hit me."

Jen stood quietly to the side. As Inman scribbled some notes, Walker fished his cell phone from the pocket of his black pants. She hadn't heard it ring and realized it was on vibrate. From his side of the conversation and the way his eyes narrowed, she deduced that he was talking to someone about the man he believed had killed Holly.

Jen wanted to grab his hand and not let go, but she didn't want to show how truly rattled she was, especially after her quasi-meltdown with the mentally ill patient. Instead, she tried to shake off the almost-paralyzing fear that had gripped her for those minutes before she knew Walker wasn't shot.

She felt sick. What if that bullet had hit him in the neck or some other unprotected area?

Inman waited patiently while Walker finished his call. A moment later, he flipped his phone shut then began his debrief. When the commander had what he needed from Walker, he moved on to Jen.

Trying to calm her jitters, she shifted her attention to him and answered his questions. It didn't take long. After he made sure Walker didn't need medical attention, Inman ordered the team into the van and drove away behind a couple of police cruisers.

Jen studied Walker. He was okay. She knew he was, but she couldn't forget the icy, suffocating emptiness that had spread through her when she thought he was shot. The same emptiness she had felt the first time Mark disappeared.

She swallowed hard, forced to admit what she'd been mentally dodging for some time. She was head over heels for Walker McClain.

They each carried their own gear and vests as they moved toward his SUV. Walker gestured to his phone. "That call was from the owner of Star Pawn, one of several store managers I asked to keep an eye out for Holly's necklace or a guy matching the description of her killer. He said a man with a scar across the knuckles of his right hand was in his shop right now. And from the info he's gotten so far, he knows the guy is homeless. Would you go down there with me?"

"Are you sure you feel up to doing this?"

"Yes, but even if I didn't, I have to go now."

She understood his urgency. There was no telling how

long the man in question might stay put. "All right. If you'll take some ibuprofen and let me drive."

"Let a gorgeous woman chauffeur me around?" He grinned. "Deal."

She smiled, taking the keys he dug from his pocket. As she opened the driver's-side door, she squashed the urge to throw her arms around him and hug him the way she'd wanted to since learning he was all right.

Following his directions, she drove toward I-35, glad all over again that he was riding with her and not in the back of an ambulance. His cell phone rang and he answered, mouthing that the caller was his brother.

"It was me and I'm okay," he said. "A hostage was hit and he's on his way to the hospital." He paused to listen.

"I will. I'll call them right now." Walker kept his gaze on Jen. "Yeah, she's fine."

A few seconds later, he disconnected.

Thanks to the lights blazing from the side of the highway, she could see lines of strain around his mouth. "How did Collier know something had happened?"

"Kiley heard through dispatch that a hostage and a SWAT medic had been shot." His voice grainy with fatigue, he dragged a hand down his face. "They knew you and I were on call."

It was nice that Collier had checked on her, too. She took the ramp for I-35 South as Walker placed a call to his parents.

Once he had reassured them multiple times, he said goodbye. He reached over and squeezed her knee. "Good work on that patient."

"It was mostly you, but thanks." Her gaze dropped to his torso, knowing his injury had to hurt, but glad the force of the bullet hadn't fractured or broken any bones. "It was hard to leave you and Tierney behind."

"You followed procedure. You don't stop for anyone who's dead or anyone who isn't bleeding critically."

"I don't have to like it."

One corner of his mouth hitched up.

"How's your chest?" she asked.

"Feels like a concrete block is crushing it, but it could be worse."

Jen was all too aware of that.

They were about two miles from their exit when his cell phone rang again. He checked the LED screen. "It's the pawnshop owner again. This can't be good."

After a brief exchange, Walker cursed, drawing a quick look from Jen. "How long ago did he leave?"

She frowned.

"Do you have any video surveillance for your store?" A pause, then, "Thanks for the call."

"What's going on?" Jen asked as he snapped his phone shut.

"The bastard took off." His voice was rough with frustration. "The store owner doesn't have any security video, so I can't get a look at the SOB. There's no sense in going down there."

"All right." She took the next exit then looped around under the overpass to get back on the highway and travel north toward Presley.

"It feels like I'm chasing the wind." He pinched the bridge of his nose. "Like I'll never find this scumbag."

There had been a time when Jen would have wondered what he planned to do if he found the man, but she knew now. Without a doubt, Walker would call the police. He would not take matters into his own hands.

She hated the discouragement in his voice. "I wish I could say something to reassure you."

"Thanks."

She felt his gaze on her, intense and thoughtful. As though he could see the nerves that were still shimmering just beneath her skin.

She was tempted then to tell him the truth about everything—about being undercover, her feelings for him. Her certainty that he wasn't the Payback Killer, despite how things appeared. But pure selfishness and maybe a hint of desperation held her back.

When she confessed, she also wanted to tell him the identity of the Payback Killer. Intentionally or not, the vigilante had thrown suspicion on Walker. He should have the satisfaction of knowing who.

And, Jen secretly hoped that sharing the identity of the real killer would cushion the blow when she did tell Walker the truth. Enough so that he might be able to forgive her and move past the betrayal he would be sure to feel. She didn't want to give him up. Not now, not ever.

As they pulled into her apartment complex, Walker seemed to have gotten past his close call, but she hadn't and she knew why.

Because she could've lost him. The thought hammered at her. As he helped transfer her gear from his vehicle to hers, her emotions skittered with lightning speed from fear to relief to a realization of how deep her feelings went.

"Thanks for agreeing to go with me to the pawnshop." His quiet voice drew her from her thoughts.

"You're welcome." If things had gone differently at the standoff, if Walker had moved in any direction, he could be dead. The thought of him leaving her tonight was too much.

She closed her Jeep door, her words coming out in an unsteady rush. "I was really scared when you got hit."

"I'm all right."

"I know. I know that." But she needed to feel for herself. She reached out a hand.

He took it, pulling her to him. "I'm fine. Don't I feel fine?"

"Yes." She skimmed her hands over his shoulders, down his arms. "Very fine."

He lowered his head and brushed her mouth with his, then curled a hand around her nape and took the kiss deeper.

When he drew back, she slid her arms loosely around his waist, whispering, "Stay with me tonight."

His body went rigid beneath her hands. "You said you weren't ready for more and that's okay."

"I changed my mind."

His gaze flared hotly. "Jen—"

She hadn't planned to ask, hadn't even thought about asking, but it felt right. She had never felt this way about anyone, like she'd found a piece of life she didn't know was missing. She needed him and she thought he needed her, too. "Please."

A muscle clenched in his jaw. "Darlin', you need to be sure."

"I am." She took his face in her hands and kissed him gently.

He searched her eyes and saw the same need that was burning inside him. "Okay."

He kept his fingers linked with hers until they reached her front door. As she fumbled the key into the lock, he slid the band from her braid and unplaited the thick cloud of her hair, dipping his head to bury his face in the silky tresses.

"I love your hair down," he murmured.

They stepped inside and she flipped a switch that turned on the lamp in the far corner. His mouth covered hers and he kicked the door shut. Their hands tangled as they took off their guns and holsters and placed them on her small breakfast table. Still kissing her, Walker slid an arm around her waist and brought her up against him, ignoring the painful throb in his chest.

She slid her hands into his hair, her fingers curling against his scalp. Her tongue was silky and hot along his. He tried to calm the rush of deep, dark need, but it wasn't happening.

Her scent, of flowers and woman and musk, swirled around him. Tugging her cotton shirt out of her pants, he slid his hands beneath to warm flesh, soft as down and baby-fine.

She helped him remove his shirt, her hands kneading his shoulders, her fingers trailing carefully over his chest.

When she leaned forward and lightly pressed her lips to his already-darkening bruise, Walker felt an ache that went deeper than the injury. Wanting to touch every inch of her at once, he got her T-shirt off and breathed out a curse at the sight of her. Lush, creamy breasts strained against the plunging white lace bra she hadn't had time to change before the call-out.

"It's a good thing I didn't see this before we worked that hostage situation," he said hoarsely. "I would've been useless."

Fighting off a growing urgency, he ran the backs of his fingers over the swell of her plump flesh touched with gold from the room's soft light. Her breathing broke, and savage need shot through him. He noticed a dime-sized scar along the inner curve of her left breast and brushed his thumb over it. "This looks like a burn."

"It's from an ember going down my turnout coat." Her voice was smoky and she trembled as she watched his hand on her. "I was suited up, working a fire, so I couldn't undress to get to it. I had to put it out quickly to keep it from burning as it worked its way down."

It happened to a lot of firefighters, but the thought of a cinder searing her tender skin jolted Walker. He bent and ran his tongue along the edge of her bra, over the mark. She tasted creamy and sweet.

Her hands delved into his hair, a small sound breaking from her when he thumbed open the front catch of her bra.

He went still inside as he stared at her perfect rose-and-cream flesh. Cupping her in both hands, he strummed his thumbs over her taut nipples. "You are stunning."

Gripping his hips, she shifted restlessly against him. "Walker."

"Give me a minute," he murmured. "I want to look at you. Besides, I won't last long once you put your hands on me." He bent and closed his mouth over her.

Making a sound that was half moan, half gasp, she clutched at his shoulders, saying breathlessly, "I have to sit down or…something."

"Bedroom?"

"Okay." Taking his hands from her breasts, she led him down a short hallway into her room.

Her flirty scent was stronger here, making his arousal rock hard. A mahogany, queen-sized bed dominated the room. Light from the hall skimmed over a small vanity with a mirror and a tall four-drawer dresser against the far wall. Moonlight slid around the drawn blinds.

She looked uncertainly at the bed, done in soft blues and greens. Pillows in darker shades of those colors were piled high on the mattress. "How can we do this so it doesn't hurt you?"

He eased down on the edge of the mattress and pulled her to stand between his knees. "We'll figure it out."

A quick tug had her bra falling to the floor. He unzipped her pants and dragged them down her lean thighs. His pulse jacked up when he saw the tiny panties that matched her bra.

At the stark hunger in his eyes, Jen swallowed hard. The deep flush of arousal streaked across his cheeks as he stared at her with an arrested expression on his face. No one had ever looked at her with such appreciation. Or heat. "Walker?"

"You're perfect."

She laughed. "You think that because you haven't had sex in a long time— Oh!"

Her words were cut off when he leaned forward and nipped a spot just below her hip bone. The room spun and she clutched at his shoulders.

"I think that because you are."

Are what? She couldn't remember what they were talking about and didn't care. Her legs shook as he guided her down to straddle his lap.

His hands spread wide across her back, holding her steady as she pressed kisses to his cheek, the corner of his mouth, his ear.

She nuzzled into his neck, biting lightly at a spot behind his ear. At the base of his nape where the corded muscles of his neck met those of his back, she touched a thin, ragged scar. "You were burned, too. From what?"

"Shooting off bottle rockets with my brother."

Rubbing at the place with one finger, she caught his mouth with hers and gently pushed at him until he laid back on the bed. The feel of her breasts against him, the velvet warmth of her skin, played hell with his control. She rose and quickly got rid of his boots and socks, then leaned over to work off his pants and briefs. Every muscle in his body tightened in sharp definition. Her breath caught.

She dragged her hands over bands of rigid muscle across his abdomen, down his strong thighs, back up to his hot, straining flesh. He was gorgeous.

She closed a hand around him and he sat up, pulling her into his lap with a growl. Nudging her head back, he raked his teeth down her petal-smooth throat and put his tongue on the place where her pulse was hammering wildly.

She shifted on his lap to arrange her legs on either side of his, then froze when he eased a finger into her silky heat. She closed her eyes, savoring how good it felt. How good *he* felt. When he added another finger, she kissed him, hard and deep.

She pushed into his touch, growing hotter and wetter. Impatient now, she started to sink down on him. Then she stopped, dropping her head against his shoulder. "I don't have any condoms."

"I do," he rasped, caressing her bottom. "In my pants pocket."

She scooted off him and grabbed the garment, pulling out a handful of foil packets. Her eyes widened. "Seven? Pretty optimistic, aren't you?"

He grinned. "I just grabbed a handful."

Tossing them on the bed, she eased back into his lap. "I thought you hadn't been with anyone since Holly?"

"I haven't." He ran his big hands up her back.

"How old are these things?"

"Not old at all." His hot tongue traced small circles on her shoulder.

"So, you've just been carrying them around, waiting for the right woman?"

"Waiting for you, and no. I got them from my brother earlier."

"Your brother!"

Walker cut her off with a kiss. "Don't worry. I didn't tell him anything. I just took them from his medicine cabinet."

Curling his fingers up inside her, he watched a deep rose

flush spread across her chest. He teased the knot of nerves between her legs until she melted around him, making a sound deep in her throat. Sweat slicked his body and his muscles coiled tight in restraint.

Together they rolled on the condom and she sank down on him, surrounding him with velvet and heat.

She whispered, "You feel amazing."

"So do you."

He looked into her beautiful blue eyes, his senses swimming with the powder-fine texture of her skin, her soft breasts teasing his chest, the fist-tight way she gloved his body with hers.

They moved together with long, slow strokes of their bodies. He pressed her hips down tight against him so he could go deeper. The surrender in her face nearly sent him over the edge, but he wasn't going until she did.

He shifted, touching her body at a higher angle until her inner muscles pulsed around him. She moaned his name, and only then did he let himself go.

Long minutes later, they lay back on the bed. She curled into his side as he caressed her shoulder.

He dropped a kiss on her hair, saying lazily, "That was the most fun I've had all day."

She laughed.

"Am I forgiven for getting condoms from my brother?"

"You caught me at a good time," she teased, kissing the underside of his jaw. "So, yes."

Her soft floral fragrance mixed with the musk of their bodies. He hugged her to him. "You haven't been with anyone since Mark?"

"No, and it was worth the wait.'

He grinned, running his hand over her taut waist down to the sweet curve of her hip. "I thought so, too."

The warm glow in her eyes went straight to his heart. This woman had come to mean so many things to him—partner, friend, lover. He had thought he would never again have what he had shared with Holly, but being with Jen felt just as right.

He had felt the same gut-deep certainty about her since the beginning, too, but he'd made excuses for it. He called it lust, loneliness, everything except what it was.

"You're quiet," she said. "Am I hurting your chest?"

"Not hardly." He slipped a hand under her hair, rubbing her nape. "I'm just tired."

"Same here." After all the excitement of their date, then the call-out, Jen was exhausted, too. The dark, spicy scent of him wrapped around her as she lay limply against him.

"I meant it when I told you I was ready to move on." His voice rumbled above her.

Touched, she snuggled into him.

He folded one arm behind his head, keeping her close with the other. "Since Holly died, I've spent a lot of time at the cemetery. That's where I was the other night when I realized I wanted you and I to be more than partners."

Jen stifled a yawn. "What night?"

"The night I helped Collier lay the patio."

She went still inside, every cell in her body vibrating.

"I went to the cemetery on my way home and stayed for a while. That's when I told her goodbye. I haven't been back since."

Tears sprang to Jen's eyes and she lifted up to give him a long, slow kiss. When she settled back down beside him, his body relaxed against hers. In seconds, his steady breathing told her he was asleep or close to it.

The cemetery, Jen thought with rising excitement. If Presley's cemetery was like most others these days, it would have security cameras. That meant she could check the footage and possibly find Walker on them. The video might provide Walker an alibi for at least one of the Payback Killer murders. And even better, she might have what she needed to prove his innocence.

She was smiling as she drifted off to sleep.

Jen woke a few hours later, spooned against Walker's front. His hand rested low on her belly, his hairy lower leg thrown over hers as though to keep her from going anywhere. Typically, she didn't like anyone on her when she slept, but it didn't bother her for Walker to be there.

Judging by the pink-and-gold light seeping in under the blinds, the sun was only now rising. She rested against the taut sinewy lines of his body, his head close to hers on the pillow. The scents of man and sex slid into her lungs.

Slowly, she turned to face him, expecting her movements to wake him, but they didn't. Even though his face was relaxed in sleep, she could see a hint of his dimples. Long, thick lashes and the dark shadow of stubble softened his lean features. She ghosted her thumb across his cheekbone, leaning in to touch her lips to his.

He squeezed her bottom and shifted, his eyes opening as he gave her a drowsy smile.

"Hey," she said.

In response, his mouth covered hers, giving her a deep, languid kiss. He slid a hard thigh between her legs. "Did I conk out on you?"

"No, I slept, too."

"How long?"

"Several hours. We were both wiped out. A lot happened yesterday."

"And last night." He threaded his fingers through her hair.

She grimaced at the painful-looking bruise on his sternum. "How does your chest feel?"

Grinning, he curved a hand around her breast. "Not as good as yours."

She laughed. "I have some things I need to do today. I'm going to jump in the shower."

"How about I wash your back?" He nuzzled her neck. "And your front."

"You talked me into it."

He rolled out of bed and scooped her up, carrying her into the restroom and putting her on her feet. Though the blue-and-white tiled space was small, it had a large shower. When Jen reached in to turn on the faucet, Walker covered her body with his and slid one arm around her waist, using his free hand to nudge her hair aside and kiss her neck.

She slipped inside and he followed, closing the door. He moved under the water with her, sliding his arms around her waist and pulling her snugly against the taut lines of his body. He was hot. And hard.

Soap-scented steam fogged the shower door. His lips teased a sensitive spot he'd found earlier on her collarbone, then he turned her, closing his hands on her waist as she met his kiss.

Water pelted his wide shoulders, slicked his dark chest hair against his torso. As his gaze burned slowly over every inch of her, she felt her body go soft.

He opened the door and reached across to the counter then shut the door, holding up a square package.

Seeing the wicked glint in his eyes, Jen laughed. "You think you're going to get lucky in the shower, McClain?"

"No, I think you are."

"Mmm, you might be right." She reached down and stroked him hard, once, twice.

He took her mouth again, his hands sliding over her breasts.

By the time they rolled on the condom, Jen was ready to melt all over him.

Long minutes later, after their pulses had slowed, Walker left Jen to dry her hair while he went to dress. She finished and walked to the door, tightening the belt of her terry-cloth robe.

Wearing only his black pants, he stood on the other side of the bed, his back to her. She started to walk over to him when he turned.

He held up her cell phone, angling the wide screen toward her. "An alert went off on your phone. I thought you had a voice mail so I was going to bring the phone to you." He watched her carefully. "Wasn't a voice mail. It was a reminder that you have a meeting later."

She knew what was coming before he said it and her stomach knotted.

"About the Payback Killer investigation. What does that have to do with you?"

Chapter 11

She'd been wanting to tell him the truth; now was her chance. She took a deep breath. "I was sent in undercover to find out if someone at Station Three is the Payback Killer."

"Undercover? Undercover for who? The cops?"

"For the fire department's Bureau of Investigations."

"So, you've been investigating someone?"

"Yes."

"The cops have questioned all of us. Who specifically are you investigating?"

Her heart slammed into her chest. "Walker—"

Whatever he saw in her face had him going still, then realization spread across his face. "Me. You're investigating me!"

"Let me explain."

"You're freakin' Internal Affairs."

She winced at the hostility in his words.

"How long have you been spying on me? Since you started at my firehouse?"

"Yes."

"So, you think I'm the Payback Killer." The dark fury in his face sent a quiver through her.

"No, I don't."

"No? Then why are you investigating me? Posing as my partner?" His voice rose, the words cracking the air like gunshots. He threw her phone on the bed. "If you don't think I killed and burned those four men, why are you watching everything I do? Exactly what have you done to investigate me?"

She wanted to look away, but she didn't. "Watched your house."

"You staked out my house?" His voice turned flinty. "When?"

"The night you were at your brother's, laying the patio." He felt betrayed. She understood that. She had to convince him to listen to her. "Please let me explain."

"What else?"

Her voice came out tinny, sounded far away. "I searched your locker at the firehouse."

He cursed. "There were a couple of days I thought I smelled your scent there, but I figured it was because I couldn't get you out of my head, not because you were *invading my privacy.*" His lips twisted. "Where else did you look?"

She managed to sound calm, despite the apprehension ripping at her. "Your SUV."

"My house?"

"No."

"Didn't have time yet?" he jeered.

She waited.

Comprehension swept across his hard features and his eyes turned blade sharp. "The night of the shift party, I caught you in the hall. You weren't looking for the bathroom. You were snooping."

There was no point denying it. Seeing the betrayal and hurt in his eyes had bitter remorse slashing through her. She'd known it would hurt, but not this deeply. Not so completely.

"I thought the fire department's IA division handled things like background checks."

"Typically, that's true." To hide her shaking hands, she jammed them into her pockets. "Because the fire chief began to suspect one of his firefighters was the vigilante, he felt he couldn't conduct an impartial investigation. And he couldn't assign one of his fire investigators to do it, either."

"Because one of them is my brother."

She nodded. "Chief Wheat went to Fire Marshal Burke with the police chief. Since the killings were classified as fire murders, Presley PD was already involved."

"So why did the rat squad choose me?"

Pain lanced her at the contempt in his voice. It shouldn't have. She'd faced coworkers' opinions about internal affairs before. Most felt that way, whether they had anything to hide or not. She swallowed hard, wary of the anger teeming beneath his icy calm demeanor, but she had to make him understand. "Burke had valid reasons for putting me with you."

"You mean, to treat me as a suspect," he said savagely.

"It's no secret that the man who murdered your wife and baby hasn't been caught and you're actively looking for him. That's motive for you to go after other slimeballs who have dodged justice. The Payback Killer's victims have all been career criminals who served time for violent acts and committed more after their release from prison. Men who showed no hope of being rehabilitated, who would've gone on hurting decent people, like Holly."

At the mention of his wife, Walker's eyes turned murderous. His body was so rigid the lines of his muscles showed in sharp definition from his biceps to his flat abs.

Swallowing hard, Jen continued, "There's also the matter of means and opportunity. Flashbangs have been used to start fires on all the dead bodies. Only SWAT and its medics have access to those stun grenades."

"*Legitimate* access," he bit out.

"Yes," she conceded, her stomach so knotted up she was nauseous. "It also didn't look good that the murders started on the anniversary of your wife's and the baby's murder."

"The *two-year* anniversary," he corrected hotly. He folded his arms across his chest, a chest she'd kissed and touched only minutes ago. The bruise was now a hideous purple-black. "Why do you think I waited two years to start taking out these skanks?"

"*I* don't think that," she said quietly. "I don't think you've killed anyone and I haven't for some time now."

"Answer me." His eyes went to cold steel.

"It's possible the anniversary date could've been a trigger. A reminder that another year has gone by and the man who murdered your wife and child hasn't paid for his crime."

"Is that your theory as to why I'm the Payback Killer? So I can make sure some of these scum will see justice?"

"I know you didn't murder anyone."

"Even though I think the Payback Killer has been doing society a favor?"

"Yes." She pressed her lips together to stop their trembling. "I had orders to look at you, Walker. You had motive, means and opportunity."

"I also have alibis."

"But the cops didn't have anything substantial enough to justify questioning you."

"They—*you*—still don't."

"That's right." For the first time, she took a step toward him.

"What makes you so sure I'm not the vigilante?"

Because I know you! She choked back the words and kept to the facts. "There's no evidence."

He moved away, his expression so scathing, it hit her like a blow. She wrapped her arms around herself, wishing she could numb the hopelessness knifing through her.

"You reeled me right in, didn't you?" The loathing in his voice almost had her recoiling. "You're damn good, but you're not good enough to prove I'm the Payback Killer."

"That's because you aren't," she said firmly. "Like I said, I haven't thought so for a long time. We can figure out who is, though. That's what I've been trying—"

"*We* can figure it out? Forget it. That's *your* job, sweetheart."

"That's right. I've been doing my job."

"I get it," he snarled. "What I'm wondering is how far you're willing to go to get it done. Is there any line you won't cross?"

The emotions churning inside her compounded into a burning knot of fury. The sheer force of it left her unable to speak for a moment. When she did, her voice was hoarse. "Don't even go there. I slept with you because I wanted to. Because I care about you. After what happened at last night's call-out, I needed you and I thought you needed me, too."

"First you weren't ready, then you were. I should've been more suspicious when you asked me to stay the night, but

I was so hot for you, nothing was working above my belt. Hoping I'd confess during a little pillow talk?"

The words tore at her like claws. She clenched her fists, saying through gritted teeth. "I did not lie to you in bed and I didn't lie to get you there."

His eyes suddenly narrowed to slits. "Are you planning to talk about us in your damn meeting?"

"No! I would never do that!"

"Have you recorded the times we've been together? Any of our conversations?"

"No! Stop making last night part of this."

"You're the one who did that."

She flinched. "Just because I didn't tell you certain things doesn't mean I lied about everything."

"Then why not tell me the truth before we got naked?"

"I thought about it, but I wanted to be able to give you the identity of the killer when I told you."

"Didn't you think it might be more important to level with me before we got horizontal? Why wait? Did you think my having that information would cushion the blow of finding out the woman I just slept with, who I thought meant something to me, has been lying to me?"

"Not telling you the truth before we slept together was a judgment call and obviously a bad one." She didn't know how to make him understand. Or even if she could. "I made a mistake, but it's not like I *planned* to sleep with you."

"When we went upstairs last night, you knew exactly where we were headed. You could've told me then."

"If I had any doubt about your innocence, I wouldn't have gone to bed with you."

"Well, give you a medal," he sneered.

"I know you're angry that I didn't tell you the truth. I know you feel betrayed and I'm so sorry I hurt you. But I wanted to be with you because I—" *Love you.* "—I care about you. What happened between us was about us and nothing else. Don't try to tell me it didn't mean anything."

A muscle ticced in his jaw. "Who knows you're a plant? Captain Yearwood? Fire Chief Wheat?"

He didn't try to tell her their night together meant nothing. He wouldn't even acknowledge what she'd said! "Yearwood doesn't know anyone is undercover. Chief Wheat does. The only people who know about me are Fire Marshal Burke and the two detectives assigned to this case."

"Who are they?"

"Jack Spencer and Robin Daly."

The lines of strain around his eyes got deeper. "Do you have any leads at all?"

She shook her head.

"Other suspects at the firehouse?"

"One, Farris. But he's been cleared."

"Why were you looking at him? Because he works at the homeless shelter where all the victims have visited at least once?"

"Yes, and that's the only connection we found for him."

"Lucky me."

"Now I might have what I need to prove you're not the Payback Killer."

"What would that be?"

"The night of the fourth murder, you said you were at the cemetery." Saying goodbye to Holly. For me. "They probably have security cameras there, and if so, you might be on them."

"Good thing I spilled my guts last night, huh? Don't you want to know where I was on the nights of the other murders?"

"Yes," she said quietly. All hope of them getting past this drained out of her. "Please tell me."

He made a sound of disgust, stalking around the bed to jerk on his socks and boots.

"Whatever you say, I'll believe you."

He stood, marched back around the bed. "I was tracking down those guys to kill them."

She pressed a trembling hand to her mouth, trying not to cry. "Walker, please."

"There's my confession. Take that to your damn meeting," he snarled, getting right in her face.

He was breathing hard, just like she was. Why did that make her ache?

"I already told you I was at the cemetery on one of those nights."

She only wanted to help him. Why couldn't he cooperate? "What about my first day? You showed up late."

His expression was so cutting it could've peeled skin. "Cemetery again."

"Had you been there all night?"

"You're interrogating me! You got a badge I don't know anything about?"

"Just tell me."

His jaw locked. Still bare-chested, he started toward her bedroom door, digging his car keys from his pants pocket.

Jen put herself in his way. She wanted to touch him, but she knew better. She kept her hands in her pockets. "Walker, I know you're hurt. And furious, but I don't believe you're the Payback Killer and I plan on proving it."

His gaze lasered right through her. "You should tell Burke your cover's blown. He'll want to assign someone new to spy on me."

Panic fluttered, fear that she'd lost him forever. "You can't tell anyone about me or the investigation. Please."

He said nothing, just stared.

"You aren't the vigilante. That means someone else in the firehouse or on the SWAT team is."

"Fine." He slashed a hand through the air. "I'll keep your damn secret, but I won't be your SWAT partner anymore. If you don't tell Inman to switch you to someone else, I will."

She nodded, her entire body pulsing with pain as though her nerves were laid bare and flayed. "I know you think I betrayed you. I would feel the same way, but I was hoping you could forgive me."

The savagery on his face told her it wouldn't happen. "Doesn't it mean anything that I'm certain of your innocence?"

"It might have, before last night." His shoulder brushed hers as he hooked a thumb at the condoms still on the bed. "You can keep those. You might need them for your next assignment."

Hope shattered inside her. Tears burned her eyes. She followed him into the living room and saw him reach down, snatch up his black T-shirt from the floor.

An icy numbness seeped into every pore. As he opened her apartment door, alarm raced through her. He was leaving, walking away. Trying one last time, she covered the distance between them. "I never meant to hurt you, Walker."

"I'm just collateral damage, right? I imagine you've dealt with it before." The look he gave her was brutal enough to have her gripping the wall for support. "I'm sure you won't lose any sleep over it."

Sleep? She stood to lose something much more important.

Fifteen minutes after leaving Jen's apartment, Walker was on his brother's front porch. It was early, but he figured Collier would be up. Staring at the horizon lined in the shimmering gold sunrise, Walker balled his hands into fists.

He hadn't gotten out of her parking lot before he was hit with her brain-melting scent. She'd been in the vehicle last night, but Walker couldn't believe how strong the fragrance was. It had his gut in knots before he snapped to the fact that he had mistakenly picked up her T-shirt in the living room. Wadding it up, he had hurled it to the very back of his SUV.

He didn't want any reminders of her, but there they were. He understood why she couldn't go around telling people she was undercover. He didn't understand why she hadn't told *him* before they'd gotten busy in her bed. The thought of her deception, her lies, had anger and resentment and hurt boiling up all over again.

He wanted to smash his fist into the wall, wanted to break something. Instead, he stabbed at his brother's doorbell.

He didn't want to think about the hurt he'd also seen in her eyes when he'd accused her of sleeping with him in hopes of getting past his guard. Didn't want to remember how many times she had said she believed he was innocent. Hell, he *was* innocent!

The front door opened and the welcoming smile on Collier's face faded. He stepped back, motioning Walker inside. "What's going on?"

Walker closed the door and followed his brother to the kitchen. He dragged a hand down his face, his whiskered jaw reminding him he hadn't shaved this morning. Reminding him of more than that.

Collier was dressed in the standard-issue navy pants and white shirt of his uniform. Striding to the counter beside the sink, he lifted the coffeepot. "Want some?"

"No, thanks. Where's Kiley?"

"In the shower." Collier poured himself a cup of the steaming brew then set the glass pot back on the burner. "What's happened?"

"Jen works for internal affairs." The fire department might call it the Bureau of Investigations, but it was still IA.

His brother frowned. Like Walker, Collier wouldn't immediately assume that her working for that division meant there was a murder investigation going on, let alone an *undercover* investigation. Not when the department typically handled background checks for potential recruits and complaints against firefighters. If needed, they also investigated suspicious fires or aided smaller fire departments.

Walker thought back over how friendly Jen had been, how she'd worked to become his friend. She'd done that for the sole purpose of getting close to him. Spying on him.

"She was put undercover to investigate me."

Collier choked on his coffee. "Undercover! What the hell?"

Walker had heard of IA departments in cities like Tulsa running undercover operations, but never Presley. Evidently, Collier hadn't, either. Walker relayed the information from Jen about how the fire chief had requested that the fire marshal investigate a couple of firefighter suspects. "They think I'm the Payback Killer."

His brother's eyes narrowed and Walker could see his fire cop gears turning. "Because you're on the SWAT team and have access to the flashbangs."

"Right. And because, according to *her*," he said acidly, "I want to make sure other scum like Holly's killer don't escape justice like this bastard has so far."

She'd said she wouldn't have slept with him if she believed he was the Payback Killer. Had she really held back from the truth because she didn't believe he was a cold-blooded murderer? Or had not telling him just been an attempt to get information via more intimate means?

He had no reason to believe Jen had slept with him for any reason other than getting under his guard and trying to work him so he might confess. And yet he couldn't forget the look in her eyes last night when she'd learned he hadn't been wounded by a gunshot. That kind of relief, the tremulous emotion in her eyes couldn't be faked. Could it?

How the hell did he know? He'd never dealt with anything like this, like *her,* before.

Collier set down his coffee cup and leaned against the counter. "How did you find out?"

"An alert sounded on her phone. I picked it up, thinking she'd gotten a voice mail. When I saw that it was a reminder for her to attend a meeting later today about the Payback Killer, I asked her about it. It all went to hell from there."

"You saw it on her phone?"

"At her apartment about fifteen minutes ago."

A shrewd light came into his brother's eyes. "Since I know that hostage situation ended several hours ago, I guess you weren't there for work."

"That's right."

"With the way the two of you acted here last night, I thought maybe y'all had already done that."

Walker didn't want to think about last night—the velvet glide of her skin beneath his hands, his mouth. Didn't want to think about her in any way except as a spy trying to bring him down. "She's the biggest mistake I've made in a long time."

"Does she have any evidence against you?"

"No, and she says she wants to prove my innocence."

Collier arched a brow. "Can she?"

Walker thought about her saying she could check security footage from the cemetery. He could do that, too. Except, why should he? He wasn't guilty, dammit. "She can't prove jack right now."

"Does it count for anything that she wants to try?"

"What? You think I should give her points or something?"

"No, just asking."

"It doesn't count for a whole lot," he gritted out. He'd thought he might be in love with her, a woman who had been scrutinizing him like a bug under a microscope, who possibly believed he was a ruthless, brutal killer. Hell, no, it didn't count.

Collier drummed his fingers on the countertop. "If she doesn't believe you're the killer, does she have any idea who is?"

"No. She said it's someone at our firehouse or on the SWAT team." Walker pinched the bridge of his nose, saying derisively, "She wanted to make sure I'm going to keep my mouth shut about who she really is and what she's doing."

"That would be the best thing to do."

"If the killer is a firefighter or on the SWAT team, he needs to be caught. I won't blow her cover even though I think Captain Yearwood has a right to know."

"Maybe so, but you shouldn't be the one to tell him."

"I know." He clenched his fists, wanting to hit something. "I hate the thought of sitting on my butt doing nothing when I should probably be trying to help myself."

"You don't need to help yourself. You haven't done anything wrong. Still, I know it won't be easy to wait and see how things shake out." Collier shook his head, regret in his eyes. "I'm sorry. Kiley and I were really hoping Jen was the one you could move forward with."

So had Walker. An image flashed of the stark pain in her eyes when he'd accused her of sleeping with him in hopes of learning something incriminating. When he'd fired off that cutting remark about her using the condoms for her next case.

He didn't want to remember the hurt he'd seen. He had enough of his own to deal with. Besides, he was the wronged party, not her.

His brother studied him for a minute. "Her reason for not telling you the truth is valid."

"I understand the reason. What torques me off is that she didn't tell me when she should have."

He was too hurt, too angry, to care if her rationale was sound or not. His problem wasn't that she had been following orders, although he didn't like it. He got that. And he got why she hadn't been free with the information she was undercover. It only made sense to keep that information a secret from the firefighters.

But she hadn't *slept* with any of them. Hadn't insinuated herself into one of their lives and made herself the brightest part of it. She'd rekindled something inside him that had been missing since Holly and the baby had died.

"Can you work with her until this operation is wrapped up?" Collier asked quietly.

"If I have to." Walker shoved a hand through his hair. "I'll work with her at the firehouse, but I told her I want to partner with a different SWAT medic. If she doesn't talk to Inman, I will."

"And that's it?"

"That's it." What else was there? "I'm staying as far away from her as possible."

It was a damn good thing he'd found out the truth about her before he'd gotten involved. It might have been just as hard to recover from losing her as it had been when he'd lost his wife and baby.

He thought about the caring way Jen had looked at him last night, how shattered she'd seemed this morning when he confronted her with the alert on her cell phone. Remembering her earnest, fervent insistence that she believed he was innocent and she wanted to prove it dimmed his anger.

He didn't want to feel anything *except* anger. It was the only thing pushing him past the pain.

He couldn't forget that she'd tried to nail his ass for being a killer. Right now, she was probably turning over the information she'd gathered on him to someone who would keep trying.

The idea that he thought he might have loved her had anger stirring all over again. He cared about her, but he wasn't in love with her. He'd let his guard down. He wouldn't do it again.

Jen had watched Walker leave from her living-room window and somehow managed to keep from going after him. It wouldn't have made any difference anyway. The bleak, dead look in his eyes as he'd walked out told her he would never get past what she'd done.

It didn't matter that her reason for not telling him the truth was motivated by good. What mattered was that she had put the investigation ahead of their relationship.

Their relationship.

That was the problem right there. She'd been an idiot to get involved with him and an even bigger idiot for sleeping with him before telling him about her assignment. He hadn't taken things to the next level with her until he'd worked out his guilt over wanting someone besides his wife and his conscience was entirely clear. Jen should've cleared hers, too.

Losing him, losing his trust, was something she might never get over. He said he'd told his wife goodbye for her. Regret gnawed deep and spread.

She knew he cared about her. It had been in his voice, his eyes, the way he'd touched her last night, but now…

Angry tears burned her eyes. She loved him, and she'd probably lost him because she had kept the truth from him. She couldn't change what had already happened, but she could show him she had been honest when she said she believed he was innocent of the Payback Killer murders. To do that, she had to find the firefighter or cop who had killed and burned four criminals.

After Walker drove away, she had picked up her black T-shirt off the floor and started to her room to put on some clothes. It had taken her a few seconds to register that the dark male scent she thought she imagined was real and actually coming from the T-shirt. *His* T-shirt.

If she had his, that meant he had hers. A knot had settled in her chest and she was suddenly hit with the sense of everything she'd lost. Oddly, burying her face in his shirt and breathing him in fired up her determination to prove him innocent of the Payback Killer murders.

After dressing, she went straight to Presley Memorial Gardens. She waited over an hour for the grounds office to open, then nearly screamed when a soft-spoken older woman told her the security cameras had been down for a few days. She would have to go through them to see if she had tapes for the dates Jen needed, and would be happy to deliver whatever was found.

Hoping, praying Walker would be on at least one of those tapes, Jen left a list of the dates of the Payback Killer murders, as well as her cell phone number and the PD's number with Detective Daly's extension.

As she drove away from the cemetery, she called Robin and Jack to break the news that Walker now knew the truth. When they asked how he had discovered she was undercover, she explained in general terms that revealed nothing of their relationship. Both detectives earned huge points when they didn't jump on her for getting personally involved with the suspect.

Even after she told them she thought Walker was innocent and she might have found proof at the cemetery. While she waited on the security footage, she wanted to take another look at the Payback Killer homicide files. Jack and Robin couldn't meet her until later, but both emphasized the importance of the first victim in serial crimes.

That was the place to look for anything that stood out from the other murders. Reviewing the Payback Killer homicide reports would help Walker and maybe keep her mind off what had happened between them.

Twenty minutes later, she sat at Daly's desk with a cup of coffee and a stack of files. Victim number one had been killed six months earlier, on the two-year anniversary of Holly McClain's murder. This first victim had been convicted of murdering a twelve-year-old girl, served seventeen years, then had mistakenly been released thanks to a computer glitch. Two days later, a twelve-year-old female was found dead outside Oklahoma City. The convict's DNA had been all over her, but before he could be apprehended, he became the Payback Killer's first victim.

Pictures of both girls were in the man's file. One had blond hair and freckles; the other was dark-haired with dark eyes. The blonde, the victim of the initial murder, looked familiar, but Jen couldn't place her. And her name, Beth Roberts, didn't ring a bell, either.

Jen continued reading the reports and notes in the file. Just days before her murder, Beth had moved to Oklahoma with her mother and stepfather. The stepfather's name leaped out at her. Trying not to get ahead of herself, Jen scanned the notes and saw the stepbrother's name. She grabbed Beth's picture for another look.

Her last name was different from her stepbrother's, but Jen knew now where she'd seen Beth Roberts's picture before. Trying to rein in her excitement, she reached for the desk phone to call Daly and Spencer, and was interrupted by a young police officer delivering the cemetery's security tapes.

Ten minutes later, Jen was fighting tears as she observed a clearly identifiable Walker leave the headstone where he'd been recorded sitting for several hours. The second tape showed the same thing on a different day.

The time and date stamps gave him alibis for two of the murders. His alibis for the other two would be checked, but Jen knew they would be as solid as these.

She had to tell him.

Chapter 12

A few hours after leaving his brother's house, Walker was at the training complex, standing with most of the team about a hundred yards from the administration building. SWAT training was scheduled to begin at one o'clock. Today, their exercise was to practice navigating the crevices of collapsed buildings, bridges, tunnels and roads. Since the Murrah bombing, these drills had become a regular part of their required sixteen hours of monthly training.

The SWAT medics who hadn't been on the call-out the night before quizzed Walker about his being saved by his bulletproof vest. Tierney walked up, saying the injured hostage had come through his surgery and was in serious but stable condition.

Walker saw Inman pause at a row of water fountains outside the administration building. After getting a drink, he went inside.

It was ten minutes before one and everyone was there except Jen. Though she wasn't late, she usually arrived fifteen to twenty minutes before the designated start time. Maybe she'd already talked to Inman and told him to speed up the transfer. Or maybe she'd called in with an excuse not to come. Either way was good for Walker. So why did he feel like hell?

"McClain, your earpiece working?" Tierney's voice came over Walker's combination earpiece and microphone.

"Ten-four," he said. "Yours?"

"You're coming through loud and clear."

Tierney tested each team member's equipment the same way, then moved on to check rappelling gear.

Walker listened to a couple of the guys swap stories about fishing in Lake Arcadia.

"Hey, Lawson," Tierney said.

Walker stiffened as she walked up beside him. Her flirty fragrance had been torturing him all day, thanks to him mistakenly picking up her T-shirt this morning. Even pitching the garment to the back of his SUV hadn't helped.

"Hey, guys," she replied.

Tierney looked her up and down. "You sitting out today?"

From the corner of his eye, Walker saw her nod. He had received no word from Inman, so he and Jen must still be partners. He cut her a look, taking in her sleek khaki slacks and snug purple top.

"I need to talk to you," she said softly.

He shifted to face her, noting the lines of strain around her eyes and a wary excitement on her features. He'd said all he intended to. "Not now."

Her blue eyes flashed and her mouth tightened. She stepped a few feet away. "Please."

He joined her reluctantly. She looked fresh, feminine. He wanted to strip off those clothes and get his hands on her again. He'd told Collier things were over for him and Jen. After what she'd done, why couldn't he stop wanting her?

"I think I know who the Payback Killer is." She kept her voice low. "If I'm right, he's someone close to you."

"Hell." Quickly looking around, he pointed at the administration building, far enough away to give them some privacy. "Let's go there."

They covered the distance in silence, and Walker followed when she stepped to the side of the building. He noticed her staring at a point over his shoulder. A glance back showed Inman walking toward the training area. The exercise would start soon. Walker shifted impatiently.

Backing into the shade of the building, Jen didn't waste any time. "When I said I haven't considered you a suspect for the Payback Killer murders in a while, I meant it. That's why I went to the cemetery after we…this morning."

"And?"

"There are security tapes showing you at Presley Memorial Gardens on the nights of two of the murders. The time stamps make it clear you couldn't have killed those victims."

Okay, so she did believe he was innocent. But the way she'd kept the truth from him before they'd ended up in bed still bothered him. "Thanks for letting me know."

"There's more. I spent the morning going through the Payback Killer homicide reports. In the file of the first victim, Kern, I found pictures of the two girls he murdered. One of them was Inman's stepsister."

"*Inman?*" Shock barreled over Walker. "I've known him a long time and he's never said anything about a stepsister. About *any* sister."

"I didn't figure you'd believe me, so I brought the file. It's in my car."

The quiet hurt beneath her words had his chest squeezing. He dragged a hand across his nape. "I believe you. That's not what I meant."

She gave him a careful look before continuing, "One day at training, I picked up his helmet and noticed an old picture of a little girl inside. He told me it was a photo of his sister. It didn't strike me as odd. I used to carry a picture of Mark in my fire helmet."

Walker knew it wasn't uncommon for firefighters or cops to carry a reminder of a loved one.

"The picture I saw in the file is of that same girl, Beth. She was murdered shortly after her family moved to Oklahoma."

Reeling from the possibility his friend might be the Payback Killer, Walker tried to keep up. His voice was rough. "Why hasn't anybody noticed this before now? Spencer and Daly had to have combed through those files at least once."

Jen nodded. "The girl's last name was Roberts. According to the file, Inman's father was married to the girl's mother. She let Beth keep her biological father's name."

"I can see why Troy would want to murder Kern, but become the Payback Killer?"

"I can't prove it yet, but it fits."

It did, Walker realized. "Inman kills the man who murdered his stepsister and the other young girl. Then he starts taking other repeat offenders off the street before they hurt or kill someone again."

Jen nodded. "That's why I went back to the beginning, to see what significance the first victim had to the Payback Killer. Kern was mistakenly released because of a computer glitch. Two days later, a twelve-year-old female was found dead outside Oklahoma City with this guy's DNA all over her. Before he could be apprehended, he became the Payback Killer's first victim."

"And Inman has access to the flashbangs, as well as to

inside information about convicts who've been recently released." Walker looked over his shoulder to make sure they were still alone. "Now what?"

"I'll take the file back to the PD so I can find out what Spencer and Daly want to do. And see what they say about getting a warrant."

"You're going to need more than a theory to get one for a search."

"Robin and Jack will know what to do. I checked the cemetery's security tapes into evidence and left a note on Robin's desk for her and Jack, explaining what was going on. As soon as one of them sees it, they'll call me."

"If you're right about this, why would Inman set me up? We're friends."

"There's no bad blood between you at all? No old grudge, maybe?"

"No. In fact, he's been rock solid all the years I've known him, especially after Holly and the baby were murdered."

"Maybe the setup wasn't intentional. Whether it was or not, I thought you should know everything."

The sincerity in her blue eyes was just as strong as it had been this morning when she had explained why she hadn't told him she was undercover before they'd slept together. He might not be as furious as he had been, but he hadn't changed his mind about being with her, either. Not for the first time, he wondered if he was making his own huge mistake by walking away from her.

She turned as if to leave.

He snagged her wrist, his thumb brushing across her ultra-soft skin. "Where are you going?"

"Back to the PD." She gently tugged from his hold. "I called Inman earlier and told him I couldn't make training today for personal reasons."

Walker figured he was the reason. He was still angry, but watching the gentle sway of her hips as she walked away, a greasy ball of dread settled in his gut.

It was the same feeling he'd had the night he lost Holly and the baby. Jen disappeared around the corner of the administration building, and Walker found himself following her.

He wasn't sure exactly what he would say; he only knew he couldn't let her go like this.

Jen walked slowly down the hill, swallowing back tears. She wasn't sure what she had expected, but it wasn't this…nothingness.

Maybe deep inside, she had thought the information she shared with Walker would convince him to forgive her. She'd been wrong.

She was so focused on the grim thought that she didn't immediately register what she was seeing when her Jeep came into view. A man—*Inman*—was closing her passenger-side door.

"What are you doing?"

He jerked around, pulling his 9 mm Glock. Stunned, Jen could only stare for a second. Her own gun was under the seat in her vehicle. In his other hand was the file she'd brought. How had he even known she had it?

She had seen him heading toward the training area. He must have noticed her talking to Walker and made his way back to them, hiding around the corner of the administration building. Eavesdropping. "You can't take that folder, Commander."

"I can't let you keep it."

He looked prepared to fight for it with every ounce of his hard muscle and brawn. Trained as they were to keep their cool in volatile situations, there was no outward sign of his anxiety. But he was twitchy. Jen could feel his subtle shift from surprise to defense.

She took a step toward him. "I know about Beth. I know what Kern did to her."

"Don't come any closer, Lawson." His hard gaze assessed the area; she knew he was looking for the quickest escape route.

"It's over now." Her legs shaking, she eased in another step. "I'm not the only one who knows about you, Troy."

"I told you not to move!"

"Lawson, hold up!" Walker called out behind her.

No! Jen turned to yell a warning. Just as Walker rounded the corner, Inman lunged for her. Jerking her by the arm, he positioned her in front of him like a shield. His arm clamped tight around her throat.

Walker already had his gun out when Inman leveled his own weapon at Jen's head.

"Drop it!" both men yelled in unison.

Walker didn't blink. "Think about what you're doing, Troy. You've got a gun pointed at one of your officers. Let her go and tell me what's going on."

"You already know what's going on." His voice was hard with rage. "I heard Lawson telling you just a few minutes ago. Lay down your weapon and kick it to me."

"It's true, then?" Walker asked evenly, his green eyes narrowed. "Your stepsister was murdered by the Payback Killer's first victim?"

"That animal killed another little girl, too. Beat her to death just like he did Bethie. He never should've been released."

"You're right," Walker agreed. "He deserved what he got. All those bastards did. You saved a lot of innocent people by getting rid of those scum. But you can't keep doing this."

Jen kept her gaze on Walker's face, hoping to feel the slightest relaxation in Inman's taut muscles. His arm tightened around her throat, choking her and making her vision hazy. As the barrel drilled harder into her temple, she thought his hand might be shaking, but she wasn't sure.

Sweat slicked her palms and a numbing fear spread through her. "Walker's right, Troy. It's time to stop now."

She was glad she'd apologized to Walker when she had. There was a very real possibility one or both of them might not make it out of this.

"You've seen his file, Lawson," Inman said harshly. "You know what he did to my sister and that other little girl."

"Yes, and he should've been punished, but not by you. You can't be the one who makes that call," Walker said quietly.

The other man sneered. "Some computer glitch or crook attorney will put these monsters back out on the street, and they'll start killing people again."

The commander's arm squeezed harder across Jen's throat and dizziness swept over her.

Walker took a small step toward her and Inman. "You can't go around handing out your own version of justice."

"You might change your mind when I tell you I found the bastard who killed your wife."

Walker stilled and his gaze sharpened. "What? How?"

"That phone call you got last night from the pawnshop owner? I overheard enough of your conversation to know what it was about and I went down there to take care of the scum. He didn't deserve to live another minute. I made it to the shop in time to pick up the guy's trail. I found the SOB! He's downtown at a homeless camp. His name is Henderson. I couldn't do anything to him then because there were too many people around, but I can do it now."

"I want to talk about that, Troy." Walker's voice sounded rusty, thick with emotion. "But you have to put down the gun and let Lawson go."

"Can't do it." Inman sounded sadly resigned.

His arm relaxed enough for Jen to get a full breath. She couldn't imagine how Walker must feel to have the information about his wife's killer dangled in front of him like a carrot. Was he tempted at all to take Inman up on his offer and finally make Holly's murderer pay? If Jen were in his shoes, she couldn't say what she would do.

"How are you going to get out of this?" Walker asked. "By blaming it on me? Have you been trying to set me up?"

"No. I never meant that to happen, and I'm sorry it shook out that way."

"So, now what?"

Inman backed up a step, dragging Jen with him. "She's going to drive me out of here."

Walker's jaw locked and he moved forward. "That's not going to work."

Jen kept her eyes on him. Surely by now, at least one of their teammates had realized Inman and Walker were absent from an exercise that should have already begun.

Walker's gaze flickered behind her and she sensed someone there. So did Inman.

He yanked her around and she used the momentum to swing both feet up and plant them against the Jeep. The abrupt stop caused Inman to falter and Jen pushed off the side of the vehicle as hard as she could.

Inman stumbled back. She pivoted and landed a punch kick to his chest.

He staggered, but didn't go down. He raised his gun and for two heart-stopping seconds, she stared down the barrel. Walker dove for the commander and knocked him to the asphalt, landing a blow that dazed the other man. His gun skittered under her Jeep; the file lay beneath his outslung arms.

Dazed, she watched the entire SWAT team swarm down the hill and subdue him. As they rolled him to his stomach and pulled his hands behind his back to cuff him, she put together that they had all heard Walker's side of the conversation with Inman through their earpieces.

Walker's gaze skated grimly over her. "Are you okay?"

"Yes. How about you?"

"I'm fine." Staring down at his friend, Walker dragged a hand across his nape. "Damn."

Inman might have been the Payback Killer, but he had also been a good friend and their leader.

The blare of sirens sounded in the distance. Patrol cars and unmarked police vehicles streamed into the parking lot. She glanced at Walker, who explained, "Someone called in the situation as soon as they heard me over the mic and figured out what was going on."

She wanted to grab hold of him and never let go, but the guarded look on his face held her back. Regardless of what had just happened, things between them hadn't appeared to change.

"Thanks for saving my life." She gave him a weak smile.

"You're welcome."

She loved him, wanted to ask him again to forgive her, but she'd played her cards. Anything else was up to him.

Jen hadn't spoken to Walker since they'd given their statements at the scene. Afterward, they had driven separately to Presley PD for several interviews and to file their reports. Once Jen finished hers, she went into an interview room with Marshal Burke, Jack and Robin.

As she and the detectives laid out their case against Inman, Jen felt a pang of regret over her team commander despite his using her as a hostage. He'd crossed the line, but Jen couldn't consider him completely bad. Not after seeing how severely Kern had beaten Inman's stepsister and the other little girl.

She did have trouble working up any sympathy for Kern or any of the Payback Killer's victims. The world was undoubtedly a better place without them.

Dealing with a mix of satisfaction and sadness, she finished at the police department and drove to her apartment. Walker wouldn't leave the cop shop until he had answered all questions from internal affairs.

She stopped at the kitchen to pour a glass of wine and take it to her bedroom. Walker's dark male scent rose from the still-rumpled bedding and the black T-shirt crumpled at the foot of the mattress. The lock on her control snapped.

Tears burned her eyes and she sank down on the edge of her bed. For the first time since he'd seen the alert on her phone, Jen cried. He had saved her life, yet he might never forgive her.

After a couple of minutes, she dried her eyes with the sheet. Loss and loneliness permeated the room, piercing her with an ache so deep she knew she would never get over Walker McClain.

Her job here was done.

She and Walker were done. She had to move on.

Seeing no need to put off the inevitable, she pulled out the boxes she'd used when she moved to Presley and began to pack.

Walker had finally finished answering questions at the PD, and now he stood at Jen's door. He still wrestled with his anger, but other things had been sifting into the mix over the past few hours.

Watching her walk out of the police department had left him with a crushing sense of loss. She'd made a mistake. Who hadn't? The easy thing would be to hold on to his anger, but Walker didn't want easy. He wanted Jen.

While trying to convince Inman to let her go, to take that gun away from her head, the icy ball of rage and hurt in Walker's chest had begun to thaw.

Looking into her eyes during those moments, neither of them knowing if Inman would pull the trigger, Walker had seen her at her most vulnerable. He'd seen her feelings for him.

Even though she had slept with him knowing there was a lie between them, he knew she'd been honest about everything else. She had told the truth when she'd claimed their making love had been only about them. She cared for him, and he was hoping it was more than that. He had to know.

Staring down at her T-shirt, clutched in his sweaty hand, he knocked on her door. The feeling of being watched had him stepping back so she could see him through the peephole. Long seconds dragged by. He didn't want to have this conversation through the door, but he would.

Finally, he heard the chain slide free and the dead bolt click. The door opened and she stood there in a soft pink shirt and faded jeans, looking tired and uncertain. After the things he'd accused her of, he understood why.

Her gaze dropped to the shirt in his hand. "I guess you came by for yours. I'll get it."

"No, that's not why I'm here. I wanted to talk to you."

She hesitated, clearly wary about what he might want. "All right."

Moving back, she opened the door wider and he walked

inside. Hell, he was nervous! As she closed the door, he noted a slight puffiness under her eyes. Beneath her tan, she was pale. And her blue eyes were shuttered against him.

She slid her hands into the back pockets of her jeans. "I talked to Fire Chief Wheat about a transfer and he approved it."

His chest tightened. "Does that mean you'll be starting another IA assignment somewhere?"

"I requested a transfer out of IA. I've had enough of lying to people I—to my friends." She pulled her hands from her back pockets and crossed her arms. Her gaze searched his face. "Have you decided what to do with the information Inman gave you about Holly's killer?"

"I passed it on to the police." Walker realized that he was content to let the cops handle Henderson because of Jen. With her, he had been able to move away from only dark memories of Holly to those of happier times they'd shared. "As I was finishing up at the station, the desk sergeant told me two patrol cops found Henderson and were bringing him in. Amazingly, he still had Holly's necklace."

Jen gave him a genuine smile. "I guess you'll get it back?"

He nodded. That wasn't all he wanted back, either. He wanted Jen.

It was then he noticed a deep cardboard box against the opposite wall next to an almost-empty bookcase. Another box sat in the bathroom doorway down the hall.

His whole body shut down. "Are you packing?"

"Yes."

"No, you're not." The thought of her leaving filled Walker with near-panic and regret. Was he going to lose the woman who had made him feel again, who made him look toward the future and not back on the past? "Not without hearing me out."

With her arms wrapped around her middle, she looked vulnerable, delicate. "Look, I understand you may never forgive me for what I did. Can we not rehash this, please?"

She might have kept something from him, but Walker knew she'd been honest about her feelings. She needed to know he believed that. "You left the PD before I could thank you."

"For what?" she asked bitterly. "Lying to you?"

"For proving I wasn't the Payback Killer, especially after some of the things I said."

Wariness flickered in her eyes. "It was my job."

"Yes, but I know now that our being together had nothing to do with that."

"It didn't." Looking away, she bit her lip.

He stepped closer. "You helped me get past the dark memories of Holly to better ones. That was something I didn't know I needed. I thought I would never find another woman who would make me want to take a chance again, but I did. I want to do that with you. I want a life with you, Jen."

She blinked. "What?"

"This morning, I said some things I shouldn't have."

"You had a reason."

"That's no excuse to be cruel. I can forgive you, if you can do the same for me." He really wanted to hold her, but he knew she wasn't ready. The thought that she might never be, that he had lost her forever had Walker forging ahead.

"The reason I came after you at the training center was to tell you that not trying to work things out between us would be a mistake. A mistake I'd always regret. There was nothing I could do about losing Holly, but I can do something about losing you. Or I want to try."

Her breath caught. "Really?"

He nodded. "Don't go. Stay with me."

Those stunning blue eyes welled with tears. "After what happened to Mark, I never wanted to get close to another man. And I didn't, until you. I feel like I belong somewhere."

"You do. Here with me."

"What if you're sorry someday? Can you really forgive me for not coming clean when I should have?"

"That hurt, but it would hurt more to let you walk away."

"If I'd just told you everything before we slept together, Inman wouldn't have held us at gunpoint. It wouldn't have gotten that far." Her gaze turned fierce, imploring. "I really thought I was doing the right thing by waiting."

"I know that."

She briefly closed her eyes, relief plain on her face. "When you left this morning, I thought we were over."

He took her hand, curling it tight into his when he realized she was trembling. "You said you cared about me. Is that truth?"

"Yes. I never lied about my feelings, Walker. Never."

"I believe you." He brushed his thumb along her jaw. "Now I need you to believe me. I love you and I want to be with you. If you don't want to stay in Presley, I'll move to Tulsa."

"Yes. I mean, no." Smiling, she wiped away a tear. "I want to stay here. I love you, too."

Unable to wait any longer, he pressed her into the wall and kissed her. Long and slow and deep. Lifting his head, he skimmed his mouth over her cheekbone, her temple, making her shiver when he murmured in her ear, "How about I help you pack and you move in with me?"

She drew back, searching his eyes then pulled his head down to hers and kissed him again.

Long minutes later, they came up for air. "What do you say?" he asked.

She slid her arms around his neck and gave him a sassy grin. "I think you're about to get lucky."

He framed her face with his hands. "I already did."

* * * * *

*Rancher Ramsey Westmoreland's temporary cook
is way too attractive for his liking.
Little does he know Chloe Burton came to his
ranch with another agenda entirely....*

That man across the street had to be, without a doubt, the most handsome man she'd ever seen.

Chloe Burton's pulse beat rhythmically as he stopped to talk to another man in front of a feed store. He was tall, dark and every inch of sexy—from his Stetson to the well-worn leather boots on his feet. And from the way his jeans and Western shirt fit his broad muscular shoulders, it was quite obvious he had everything it took to separate the men from the boys. The combination was enough to corrupt any woman's mind and had her weakening even from a distance. Her body felt flushed. It was hot. Unsettled.

Over the past year the only male who had gotten her time and attention had been the e-mail. That was simply pathetic, especially since now she was practically drooling simply at the sight of a man. Even his stance—both hands in his jeans pockets, legs braced apart, was a pose she would carry to her dreams.

And he was smiling, evidently enjoying the conversation being exchanged. He had dimples, incredibly sexy dimples in not one but both cheeks.

"What are you staring at, Clo?"

Chloe nearly jumped. She'd forgotten she had a lunch date. She glanced over the table at her best friend from college, Lucia Conyers.

"Take a look at that man across the street in the blue shirt, Lucia. Will he not be perfect for Denver's first issue of *Simply Irresistible* or what?" Chloe asked with so much excitement she almost couldn't stand it.

She was the owner of *Simply Irresistible,* a magazine for today's up-and-coming woman. Their once-a-year Irresistible Man cover, which highlighted a man the magazine felt deserved the honor, had increased sales enough for Chloe to open a Denver office.

When Lucia didn't say anything but kept staring, Chloe's smile widened. "Well?"

Lucia glanced across the booth at her. "Since you asked, I'll tell you what I see. One of the Westmorelands—Ramsey Westmoreland. And yes, he'd be perfect for the cover, but he won't do it."

Chloe raised a brow. "He'd get paid for his services, of course."

Lucia laughed and shook her head. "Getting paid won't be the issue, Clo—Ramsey is one of the wealthiest sheep ranchers in this part of Colorado. But everyone knows what a private person he is. Trust me—he won't do it."

Chloe couldn't help but smile. The man was the epitome of what she was looking for in a magazine cover and she was determined that whatever it took, he would be it.

"Umm, I don't like that look on your face, Chloe. I've seen it before and know exactly what it means."

She watched as Ramsey Westmoreland entered the store with a swagger that made her almost breathless. She *would* be seeing him again.

Look for Silhouette Desire's
HOT WESTMORELAND NIGHTS
by Brenda Jackson,
available March 9
wherever books are sold.

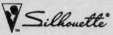

THE WESTMORELANDS

NEW YORK TIMES
bestselling author

BRENDA JACKSON

HOT WESTMORELAND NIGHTS

Ramsey Westmoreland knew better than to lust after the hired help. But Chloe, the new cook, was just so delectable. Though their affair was growing steamier, Chloe's motives became suspicious. And when he learned Chloe was carrying his child this Westmoreland Rancher had to choose between pride or duty.

Available March 2010 wherever books are sold.

Always Powerful, Passionate and Provocative.

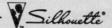

SPECIAL EDITION

FROM *USA TODAY* BESTSELLING AUTHOR
CHRISTINE RIMMER

A BRIDE FOR JERICHO BRAVO

Marnie Jones had long ago buried her wild-child
impulses and opted to be "safe," romantically
speaking. But one look at born rebel Jericho Bravo
and she began to wonder if her thrill-seeking side
was about to be revived. Because if ever there was
a man worth taking a chance on, there he was,
right within her grasp....

*Available in March
wherever books are sold.*

Devastating, dark-hearted and…
looking for brides.

Look for

BOUGHT:
DESTITUTE YET DEFIANT

by *Sarah Morgan*

#2902

From the lowliest slums to Millionaire's Row…
these men have everything now but their brides—
and they'll settle for nothing less than the best!

Available March 2010
from Harlequin Presents!

REQUEST YOUR FREE BOOKS!

2 FREE NOVELS
PLUS
2 FREE GIFTS!

ROMANTIC
SUSPENSE

Sparked by Danger, Fueled by Passion.

SRS10

HARLEQUIN
Ambassadors

Want to share your passion for reading Harlequin® Books?

Become a Harlequin Ambassador!

Harlequin Ambassadors are a group of passionate and well-connected readers who are willing to share their joy of reading Harlequin® books with family and friends.

You'll be sent all the tools you need to spark great conversation, including free books!

All we ask is that you share the romance with your friends and family!

You'll also be invited to have a say in new book ideas and exchange opinions with women just like you!

To see if you qualify* to be a Harlequin Ambassador, please visit
www.HarlequinAmbassadors.com.

*Please note that not everyone who applies to be a Harlequin Ambassador will qualify. For more information please visit www.HarlequinAmbassadors.com.

Thank you for your participation.

BAP09BPA